The Mistletoe Game

Hot Holidays Book 1

Ellis O. Day

I love to hear from readers so email me at
authorEllisOday@gmail.com

https://www.EllisODay.com

Follow me

Facebook
https://www.facebook.com/EllisODayRomanceAuthor/

Closed FB Group (sneak peeks, sample chapters, and other bonuses)
https://www.facebook.com/groups/153238782143373

Bookbub
https://www.bookbub.com/authors/Ellis-o-day

Instagram
https://www.instagram.com/authorEllisOday/

Twitter
https://twitter.com/Ellis_o_day

Join My Readers' Group and for a limited time get the entire Six Nights of Sin series for FREE

(THERE'S A PEEK OF BOOK ONE AT THE END OF THIS BOOK)

Join my newsletter to get your FREE books

Here's What You Get When You
Join My Readers' Group

Win Before You Can Buy
Exclusive Giveaways
Free Books
Sneak Peeks

Ellis O. Day

CHAPTER 1: ADRIAN

Adrian wandered through the crowd at La Petite Mort Club, enjoying the lavish holiday decorations. Over the last ten plus years, he'd grown accustomed to a Christmas filled with sand, dirt and sometimes bullets, but that was his past.

About eight months ago, his friend Mitch had convinced him to leave the Marines to work in cyber security at a private investigator firm. On most days, he was happy with his decision. The pay was fabulous and his boss, Patrick Westman, was great, but he missed the military—not the fighting or killing but the connection he'd had with his team of brothers. His phone beeped and he pulled it from his pocket.

MITCH: Running late.

He frowned at the screen. Late his ass. The bastard was hooking up.

ADRIAN: Bullshit. Who is she?
MITCH: Who knows & who cares? She's got great tits and an eager pussy.

ADRIAN: Protect your soldier.
MITCH: Always.

He slid his phone back into his pocket. He was on his own. He stopped at the bar and pushed his bottle of Bud toward the front, signaling that he was ready for another. The bartender grabbed it, too busy to chat so Adrian scanned the crowd.

Most of the people were behaving tonight—no shows on the stages, only a few couples having sex. It was quiet but the air was filled with anticipation. It could be due to the Club being closed tomorrow for Christmas–one last bang before spending time with family–or it could be the game Desiree, one of the Pleasure Associates, was organizing.

She stood on stage supervising two bouncers and a few customers as they arranged props draped in festive green, red and gold sheets on the main stage.

He paid the bartender for the beer and took a gulp. He should go home and get some rest. His family had a big party planned for tomorrow. The only reason he'd come out tonight was because Mitch had begged him. That'd teach him for doing a good deed. His friend was getting laid and he was studying Christmas sheets on a stage. It was too bad he thought of Desiree like a kid sister. He needed to get laid. His gaze skimmed over the bar and screeched to a halt on the saddest woman he'd ever seen.

She sat alone, her face pale and lips tight but it was her eyes that made his heart twist. She looked like her world had ended and he hated, absolutely hated, seeing women sad. His six sisters could attest to that. He'd taken many a punishment for things they'd done to keep them from crying.

The woman stared at her phone and then wiped her eyes, leaving a smudge of mascara on her cheek and making her look even sadder. That was it. He was going to cheer this lady up. He grabbed his beer and froze as she answered her phone, a smile spreading across her face.

"Shit," he mumbled. That smile transformed her from okay-looking to gorgeous. She had thick, honey-brown hair, high cheekbones with a wide mouth and lush, red lips that promised all sorts of pleasurable things. His dick hardened. Change of plans. He wasn't just going to cheer her up; he was going to make her smile, preferably as she gazed up at him from his bed.

Baby steps. First, he had to meet her. Then he'd fuck her. His gaze dropped to her wrist. He was both disappointed and relieved that she wasn't wearing a bracelet that marked her as a Pleasure Associate. If she had been, sex would've been a sure thing, but he did love a challenge. He made his way around the bar toward her. It was time to brighten both their nights.

CHAPTER 2: ELLIE

Ellie sat at the bar, twirling her straw in her drink as she stared at the Christmas lights and tried not to cry. She couldn't believe Marc was standing her up again, especially here. She hadn't even wanted to come to this place, but once his friend Bruce had gotten them guest passes Marc had pestered her relentlessly. She'd finally agreed to meet him at La Petite Mort Club just to shut him up. Now, she was sitting alone at the bar in a sex club and he didn't even have the decency to show up. He'd call with some lame excuse about…

Her phone beeped. It was a message from Marc. Great. Here came the lame excuse. She tapped the screen and stared at the picture of Marc and…the other woman.

They were in Marc's tiny office at the gym. The woman sat on the desk her legs wrapped around his hips as he fucked her. She held the phone over his shoulder and had smiled for the picture. Ellie should be furious but all she could think was *she's pretty*. It wasn't surprising. Marc wouldn't waste his time with someone unattractive.

Her phone rang. It was her mom. She took a deep breath, wiping at her eyes. Everything would be okay. She had her family and her job. She didn't need a man, especially one like Marc. "Hi, Mom. Merry Christmas."

"Merry Christmas, honey."

She smiled. Just hearing her mom's voice made everything okay.

"I know you and Marc have a big night planned so I'll make this quick."

"It's okay, Mom." There was no reason to explain that her big plans were now going to the grocery store for some chocolate and then home to cry. She'd tell her family about the breakup tomorrow.

"No. You two need time alone. You work too much."

"We spend time together." This was not her fault, but that little voice whispered, *Are you sure? All of your boyfriends have cheated on you. If it isn't your fault, then whose fault is it?*

"Will you two be staying over tomorrow night?" asked Mom.

"Dad would be okay with that?" Her father was not a fan of pre-marital sex.

"Of course not but let me worry about him." There was a smile in her mother's tone that made Ellie want to cry. All she wanted was a relationship like her parents had. Yes, they'd gone through a rough patch a few years ago but they'd made it through, and they seemed happier than ever.

"Uhm. Yeah, I guess we might stay over." She cleared

her throat. It wasn't really a lie. She'd spend the night tomorrow which would give Marc time to pack his stuff and be out of the apartment before she returned.

"That's wonderful. I can't wait to see you. Have fun tonight."

"Thanks. Can't wait to see you too." She swallowed a lump in her throat. She wanted her mom's hug. She needed it but she'd have to wait. She pressed the button ending the call. The picture of Marc and that woman stared up at her.

She closed the message app. The bitch was welcome to him because she wasn't going through this again. She dialed his number. It went straight to voicemail. Good. She didn't want to speak with the bastard anyway. "We're done. I want you and your crap out of my apartment by the time I get home from my parents' house tomorrow."

She hung up and dropped her phone into her purse. She grabbed her vodka and grapefruit, taking a long drink, surprised that she didn't feel anything. She should be angry, hurt, sad, something but she just felt numb. She'd wasted almost three years on the jerk and two on the cheating asshole before him. Her gut twisted with disgust but at herself not them. As of tonight, she was done with arrogant, alpha males, who moved from one woman to the next like they were nothing more than dishes on a buffet.

"Excuse me. May I buy you a drink?" asked a man with a voice like whiskey—rough and smooth at the same time.

"No. Tha…" Her breath caught in her chest. This guy was better than good looking. Tall. Dark hair. Sharp features, a sexy mouth and vibrant green eyes. Maybe she should reconsider her decision to avoid men like him but just for tonight. It'd been awhile since she'd had sex and it was Christmas Eve. He'd make a delicious package to unwrap. She forced herself not to check out the yummy one between his legs.

"Are you waiting for someone? I'll keep you company while you wait." He waved the bartender over. "Another for the lady and myself."

"I said no." Nope, she was not reconsidering. She was done with the macho, alpha male types. She'd find herself a nice, sensitive teacher or accountant like her sister had done. No, not like Trevor. Tina's fiancé was as far from macho as he could be, but he was still a jerk.

"Please, let me get you a drink. You seem sad and I'm a good listener." He smiled.

She almost melted into a puddle on the chair. It should be illegal to be that good looking. "Right." Men like him never listened; they hunted and conquered.

The bartender walked over and placed the drinks in front of them. He handed her some money before sitting on the chair next to Ellie. His gaze traveled down her body, resting a quick second on her cleavage. She breathed in his scent—subtle cologne and male. The place between her legs began to hum but she wasn't doing this again. She was done jumping from one lousy, macho jerk to the next. She was twenty-six years old. It was time to change her type. She stood.

"Where are you going?" He seemed genuinely

confused.

"I said no."

"Come on. The drinks are here. You're here. I'm here." Again, his eyes dipped to her chest. "Shame to let something so delicious go to waste."

"You're all alike. Believing a smile and a drink will get you whatever you want. Well, it won't work on me." *Not tonight anyway. Hopefully, never again.*

"Hey." He held up his hand. "I only meant to keep you company."

"Really? My company. That's all you wanted."

"Yes." One corner of his mouth turned up in a sexy smile. "At least to start."

"Asshole." She grabbed her drink and left.

CHAPTER 3: ADRIAN

Adrian couldn't keep his gaze off that woman's ass. She wore a short, black and red dress that hugged those large, round cheeks like a second skin. Her butt was perfect for his hand and she needed a spanking more than any woman he'd ever met. He shifted slightly, giving his rising cock some room.

"Hey Adrian, I didn't expect to see you tonight." Desiree stopped beside him at the bar. "I thought your family was having a big to-do for your first Christmas home?"

"They are but that's tomorrow." His eyes drifted to the woman with the honey-brown hair and those suck-me lips.

"I'm glad you're here. I need some contestants for my game."

"What are you doing up there?" He pulled his gaze away from the woman, who now sat on the other side of the bar, and glanced at the stage.

"It's the Mistletoe Game and I need you"—she tapped his arm—"to play."

"How do you play?"

"I'll explain the rules when the couples get on stage." Desiree smiled, her eyes mischievous. "I promise, you'll enjoy it."

"Sorry, but I'm single tonight."

"That's perfect because partners are chosen at random." She held out a bag. "Pick a chip."

"I'm not into games, especially ones where I don't know the rules." With his luck he'd end up tied to a spanking bench while some Domme beat his ass and that was so not his thing.

"It's La Petite Mort Club. The rules are consent and pleasure."

"Sounds fun but—"

"Please. Ethan isn't thrilled that he agreed to let me do this. I need people to participate or it'll be the last time he lets me coordinate an event."

"He has had a bit of a stick up his ass lately."

"So, you'll play?" She stared at him hopefully.

He sighed. He was a sucker for a woman in need, but after growing up with six sisters he'd learned how to negotiate. "I'll tell you what. I'll play if you make sure she's my partner." He nodded at the woman across the bar.

CHAPTER 4: ELLIE

Ellie searched on her phone for locksmiths that were open this late on Christmas Eve. She either changed her locks or she went to a hotel because she was not dealing with Marc tonight. The asshole wouldn't have the decency to stay with his slut. He'd creep into the house in the middle of the night and into her bed. That's what he'd done the last time and then he'd somehow convinced her that she was wrong about his cheating. That wasn't going to happen again because this time she had more proof than odd charges on her credit card.

"Excuse me," said a soft, feminine voice.

"Yes." She pulled her gaze away from her phone.

It was the woman who'd been on stage earlier in the evening. Ellie knew men found her attractive, but this woman was extraordinarily beautiful with wavy black hair and blue eyes.

"Hi, I'm Desiree."

"Ellie." She smiled at the other woman. She'd never been the type to be jealous of another woman's beauty.

"I know you don't know me, but I need a favor."

"A favor?" Ellie's surprise must've shown on her face because the other woman started rambling.

"This is the first event I've been allowed to organize here and"—Desiree lowered her voice—"I screwed up. I have one more man than woman. I need a partner for him in the Mistletoe Game."

"Ah…no. Thanks but I'm not in the mood."

"Please." Desiree grabbed her hand. "It'll be fun, and it'll take your mind off him."

"Who said—"

"I saw you talking on the phone. You're upset, and it's always because of some man." Desiree rolled her eyes on the last word.

"That's true." She laughed.

"So, you'll play?"

"Ah…"

"Please. I need one more woman and then I can start the game. If I take too long my boss is going to stop this before it begins." Desiree's gaze lifted to the second floor.

Ellie's eyes followed the other woman's and her mouth dropped open. The most gorgeous man she'd ever seen stood at the balustrade, watching them, his face impassive. "He looks like a fallen angel. An angry one."

"Doesn't he though." Desiree laughed. "But Ethan isn't angry, he's cranky."

"Why?"

"Woman troubles. What else?"

"Him?" Men like him didn't have women troubles, they made trouble for women.

"Yep." Desiree shrugged. "As you know, even beautiful people get their hearts broken." She touched Ellie's arm.

"Ah...sure." She didn't consider herself beautiful. Cute? Yeah. Pretty? Some days. But beautiful? No.

"Thank you. Thank you." Desiree gave her a quick hug before handing her a dark green poker chip. "I'll explain everything when I call you to the stage."

"Uhm...I didn't—"

"Don't worry. It'll be fun. I promise." Desiree grinned and started to walk away.

Ellie grabbed her arm. "What kind of game? Exactly."

"What does it matter?" Marc pushed his way to the bar, stopping at her side, his brown eyes hard with anger. "You won't play anyway."

"I see you got my message." She let go of Desiree and prepared herself for the upcoming argument. She usually backed down from Marc's temper but not this time.

"Yeah. What the fuck's your problem? I was working late because all you do is bitch about money and then I get this message from you." He moved closer. "Babe, you know I'm only working this much for you. For us. For our future."

"Please, don't." She looked around him. "Sorry, Desiree but I think you'll have to count me out."

"Fuck that. We'll play," said Marc. "That's why we're

here."

"*We* aren't doing anything. *We* are done. Over."

"Is there a problem?" One of the bouncers stepped up behind Marc.

"No. Sorry," said Marc. "Ellie"—he tipped his head—"we need to talk."

"No, we don't."

"Ellie, you know you get like this. Jealous over nothing."

"I can smell her perfume on you." This was so embarrassing. She hated being the center of attention and Marc wasn't even trying to be quiet.

"I saw my sister today. That's what you smell."

She was so not in the mood for this. "I'm done, Marc. I mean it. I'm not falling for your lies again." She didn't deserve to be treated like this.

"I'm not lying." His face began turning red with anger. "You'd better watch it because I've about had it with your jealous fits."

"My jealous…You've about had it." She was at a loss for words but luckily, she had a picture. She picked up her phone, almost smiling because she hated him right now. She couldn't wait to show him that she wasn't as stupid as he thought. "I'm glad you're *almost* done because I'm completely done"—she opened the message and shoved her phone in his face—"with you."

His eyes widened and then narrowed. "Ah…that's not—"

"Don't you dare try and tell me that isn't you." She

enlarged the picture so that the side of his face filled the screen.

"Son of a…that bitch." He pulled his gaze away from the phone and pushed her hand down. "Babe, this isn't what you—"

"Don't." She couldn't do this. "It's over, Marc." She was tired, exhausted. "I'm going home. I'll stay at my parents' house tomorrow. Be out of the apartment before I get back." She stood.

"This is your fault."

"Excuse me? How is this my fault?"

"If you weren't so fucking cold in bed, I wouldn't have to fuck someone else." His chest puffed out.

"I am not cold." Her words came out sure, but she wasn't. Every guy she'd ever loved had cheated on her. She'd always blamed them but perhaps it was her. She was a forensic accountant. She looked for patterns and she was the common denominator.

"Ha. I had to beg you to come here tonight. Sex clubs aren't your thing. Remember?" He sneered down at her. "Just like sex isn't your thing."

"I like sex." She did. "We used to have sex all the time."

"Yeah, before you froze up like a fucking iceberg." He gave her a disgusted look before turning and walking away.

She dropped onto her chair and stared at the holiday lights. She was not cold. She wasn't. This wasn't her fault. They were the ones who cheated. They were the ones who were broken. If she kept telling herself that, one day she might believe it.

CHAPTER 5: ELLIE

Ellie finished her second drink. She wanted to leave but she refused to give Marc the satisfaction of seeing her walk out alone while he was surrounded by women. She'd wait for him to go to the bathroom and then she'd sneak out like the lonely, pathetic loser she was.

"Ladies and gentlemen. It's time for La Petite Mort Club's Mistletoe Game." Desiree's voice rang through the Club's speaker system.

The crowd cheered and everyone either turned toward the stage or walked over to it.

Her eyes dropped to the green chip that sat on the bar next to her. She'd forgotten all about this stupid game. There was no way she was playing but it was the perfect time to make her way to the door. She grabbed her purse, threw some money for a tip on the bar and stood.

"Thanks. Don't forget your chip," said the bartender when she grabbed the glass empty and tip.

"Right. Thanks." She picked up the green chip and meandered along the outskirts of the crowd, pretending to

17

watch the stage but really keeping her eye on Marc who'd somehow managed to find a place at the very front with his asshole friend Bruce.

She hated him even more. He was a golden boy. Everything always went his way. It was so annoying but soon he'd be out of her house and her life. She sidled past a bouncer and started walking faster for the door. She'd go home to her empty apartment, curl into the fetal position and cry, except Marc would come home at some point tonight. She pulled her phone from her purse. She was going to a hotel. She'd order room service and watch old movies while she made herself sick on chocolate.

CHAPTER 6: ADRIAN

Adrian stood on the stage, searching the crowd for his partner. This was the second time tonight he'd almost lost her. The first had been when her boyfriend had shown up.

What an ass. He didn't care how pissed a guy got with his girlfriend; it was never okay to say that kind of shit about her, especially in a crowded bar. It'd taken everything he'd had not to walk over there and introduce his fist to the asshole's face.

His gaze landed on honey-brown hair and his eyes roamed over her frame. That woman sure did have a nice ass but unfortunately, it was heading for the door. There was no way he was letting that happen.

"Ah, Des." He waved at his friend. "My partner is trying to flee." He pointed at the woman. His woman. At least that was how he'd been referring to her in his head ever since he'd seen her smile.

"Oh. Darn. I guess she doesn't want to play." Des gave him a mischievous grin.

"She does. I'm sure." He'd winked at his friend. "If

not, I'll make her want to play." Both on stage and later in his bedroom.

"You'd better. She's had a bad night and could use a good present for Christmas." Desiree turned on the microphone in her hand.

"Oh, don't worry. I'll stuff her stocking just right." He laughed.

CHAPTER 7: ELLIE

"Ellie! Ellie!" Desire's voice boomed through the Club.

"You have got to be kidding me," Ellie mumbled as she stopped. The door was right there. Right there. She could make a run for it but everyone, including Marc, would be watching her.

"Ellie, come up here. I remember the chip you picked. You're Green." Desiree almost squealed with excitement. "Come here and meet your partner."

"Ellie? Ha. She won't play," yelled Marc. "She doesn't have the guts or desire to do anything exciting."

Her back stiffened. She refused to let him win. It was just a game. A kiss under the mistletoe or something stupid like that. She'd do this and go home.

"You hush." Desiree glared at Marc before turning back toward Ellie and smiling. "Everyone move out of her way. Let her through. Damon, help her."

A large bouncer smiled down at her, offering his arm.

He was the biggest man she'd ever seen, well over six feet tall and muscular was an understatement. He had short, dark brown hair and friendly brown eyes. "Shall we?"

"Of course." She smiled back but was sure her lips trembled. She didn't want to be on stage in front of all these people.

"It'll be fine. Des knows how to show everyone a good time." He led her through the crowd.

"That's what I'm afraid of," she mumbled but obviously not quietly enough because he chuckled.

"Don't worry." He took her hand as they approached the stairs. "Consent is the number one rule here. If there's anything you don't want to do, just say it. No one will judge you."

"Thanks." Her eyes darted to Marc. Damon was wrong about that because one person was eagerly waiting for her to back down. She'd die before she let that happen. She walked onto the stage.

The gorgeous man who'd wanted to buy her a drink grinned as he held out a green chip. Ellie's vodka and grapefruit turned to rock in her stomach. No. Not him. Anyone but him.

"I think you're my partner." The guy looked around the stage where about a dozen couples stood. He was the first in line and the only one who was alone.

She almost bared her teeth as she plodded forward. She'd kiss the asshole and go home. Hopefully, he'd have bad breath or be a horrible kisser.

"Nice to meet you, Ellie." He held out his hand, trying

not to smile but his eyes sparkled with laughter. "I'm Adrian."

"Hi, Adrian." She forced a smile. The jerk was loving this.

"Let's start the Mistletoe Game," yelled Desiree.

The crowd roared.

"One person from each team needs to pick a package." Desiree pulled a gold sheet off one of the props, displaying a wooden cross with presents, draped in holiday colored linen, hanging from it. "I'd suggest sending the person with the worst aim."

"There's going to be throwing like in baseball?" She glanced at Adrian.

He shrugged. "Don't know. Could be shooting."

"Shooting?" She frowned at him. "Inside the building?"

"Don't look at me like that." He grinned. "It's possible."

"Then I guess I pick because I've never even fired a weapon."

"Squirt gun? Nerf gun?"

"Oh. I hadn't thought of those." She smiled sheepishly at him. "I'm not much better with them than with balls. Are you any good?"

His grinned deepened as he leaned close to her. "I'm very, very good and I bet you're better with balls than you say."

"That's not what I meant." She huffed. He was a typical macho jerk, making everything sexual.

"I was talking about shooting and throwing. What were you talking about?"

"Right." She sent him a look that said clearly, she wasn't that big of a fool. "I'll pick."

She followed the others across the stage and unhooked the closest package before returning to Adrian's side.

"Everyone unwrap your present" Desiree almost bounced with excitement.

Ellie pulled the linen off the gift. It was a plastic mistletoe with a strand of spongy berries. She glanced down the stage at the others. They all had the same thing except some had more berries than others.

"Uhm, what is it?" asked one of the other guys.

"A Mistletoe. La Petite Mort Club style." Desiree beamed.

"I can see it's a mistletoe but what do we do with it?" asked the same guy.

"You'll see." Desiree grinned at them as she walked to another prop.

"You know"—Adrian leaned by her ear and whispered—"the tradition of mistletoe is that a boy gets to kiss the girl for every berry." He flicked the cluster of berries with his finger. "That's a lot of kisses."

"Six. There are six..." She turned, her breath catching when she realized that he hadn't shifted away. He was only inches from her face. If she tipped her head a little, her lips would be on his. The pulse between her legs began to throb a slow, steady rhythm, urging her to eliminate all space between them.

"Yes?" His breath tickled her cheek and lips.

She cleared her throat and ignored her desire. "Berries. There are six berries on this plant and we're not going to kiss six times." She'd combust and turn into a pile of ash because this man wasn't even cooperative enough to have bad breath and there was no way a guy who looked like he did was a bad kisser.

"We'll see."

"Let me introduce you to...Mistletoe Mary!" Desiree pulled a red sheet off another prop.

Shouts and catcalls from crowd filled the air.

"Oh, wow." She had no words.

A sex doll was handcuffed spread eagle to a stand. The doll had long, black hair, open, red lips, a body that most women would envy, and she was naked—completely—and it looked like there was a hole..."I think she's anatomically correct."

Adrian burst out laughing.

"Dang. I said that out loud?" She cringed as she cast a glance at him, making him laugh harder.

"Yes, you did but I'll have to take your word for Mary's *correctness* because I've never met her. I prefer my partners living." His eyes took a quick trip down her frame, leaving heat in their wake.

"Let's see who goes first." Desiree reached into a red, Santa bag, pulling out a chip. She held it up. "Green! Green goes first."

"And my night keeps getting better and better," she mumbled.

"At least it'll be over soon."

"Not soon enough."

"Both of you, come here." Desiree removed another sheet, uncovering a cart filled with twelve glasses each containing a liquid of a different color.

Adrian waved his hand. "Ladies first."

"Chicken," she muttered, his smile making her want to grin as she walked across the stage.

"Stop right there." Desiree pointed at the white line of tape on the floor.

Ellie and Adrian stopped.

Desiree rolled the cart until it was directly to Adrian's right. "I'm sure everyone knows that people kiss under the mistletoe, but the tradition began with a girl standing under the mistletoe. The boys would line up for a kiss, but kisses were limited to the number of berries. They'd wait in line. When they got to the girl, if there was still a berry on the plant, they'd pick it and then kiss her. As soon as the berries were gone, so were the kisses." Desiree paused. "The Mistletoe Game is based on this but"—she stressed the word—"it's been modified in La Petite Mort Club style."

The crowd cheered.

"Adrian, dip the berry into the green glass and then throw it at Mistletoe Mary but be careful where you hit her. Wherever that berry lands is where you get to kiss Ellie and you only get as many kisses as berries."

"Kiss the doll," yelled Marc. "She'll be more fun."

Ellie flipped him the bird because she couldn't pull her

eyes from that naked doll. If he hit her breast or…lower…Oh God, she couldn't do this.

"This is getting interesting," said Adrian.

"That isn't the word I'd use," she almost hissed. as she pulled her eyes away from the naked doll. She wanted to slap that sexy smirk off his face but that'd be childish so instead, she grabbed his arm. "Aim for her mouth."

"Her mouth ?" He frowned down at her. "Why would I do that?"

"A kiss. You wanted six kisses."

"And I'm going to get them." His smile was beyond wicked. "All six kisses…wherever I want on your body."

Her heart tried to beat out of her chest while the pulse between her legs was throwing a dance party.

"What are you waiting for?" shouted people from the crowd.

"Give me a minute," Adrian yelled. "I only get six. I don't want to waste any." He studied the doll as he dipped the sponge-berry into the green liquid. He raised his arm and threw.

Ellie chanted in her head—face, face, face—as the berry flew across the stage, slapping Mary right on the top of her breast.

"Yeah!" shouted the crowd.

"Shit." Her hand went to her chest. She could almost feel those lips now and then another berry flew landing on the other breast, closer to the nipple.

"Lower," shouted the crowd.

"Go for her pussy!" yelled someone and the crowd

began to chant. "Pussy. Pussy."

Good lord, she'd die if he kissed her there. On stage. In front of all these people. It'd been even longer since Marc had done that. He hadn't been a big fan of going down on her. She'd probably combust or orgasm right on stage and she couldn't let that happen.

Adrian raised his hand, his fingers dyed green from the liquid. His eyes narrowed and just as his arm started forward Ellie elbowed him in the side.

CHAPTER 8: ADRIAN

"Ouch." Adrian's arm twitched from a small, pointy elbow poking into his side.

The crowd booed as his mistletoe berry completely missed the doll.

"You missed!" Desiree sent him a disgusted look. "How could you miss?"

"Good question." He frowned at Ellie who stood by his side with an innocent expression on her pretty face. "Redo." He took a step forward. He was getting that berry and going to land it right on that doll's anatomically correct pussy.

"No. Wait." Ellie grabbed his arm, her fingers digging in so hard he could feel her nails through his suit jacket and shirt. "That's not fair. He had his shot."

"She's right," said Desiree. "Unless there was a good reason that you missed." Her eyes darted from him to Ellie.

"There wasn't. He just has bad aim," said Ellie.

"Bad aim? That's insulting. The doll is only a few feet away."

"Don't feel too bad. It happens to the best of us." Ellie stared straight ahead, refusing to look at him.

"Bad aim and bad taste," muttered her asshole ex-boyfriend.

A few others snickered.

Adrian's pique at Ellie's cheating vanished as he turned toward Marc. "Why don't you shut the fuck up?"

"Me?" Marc pointed to himself.

"Yeah, you." Adrian took a step toward him, noting that the bouncers headed through the crowd in Marc's direction.

"Why don't you make me?" Marc walked toward the stairs.

The guy moved with the confidence of a man who knew how to fight but Adrian had spent his adult life in the Marines. It'd take him less than a minute to render the guy unconscious.

"Both of you stop it." Desiree waved over one of the bouncers to block the stairs. "Adrian, you're ruining my game."

"Don't worry. This won't take long."

"Before you're out cold," taunted Marc.

"Don't. Please." Ellie grabbed his arm, stepping in front of him. "Please," she whispered. "I don't want a scene." Her big brown eyes pleaded with him and her lips were back to that tense straight line.

He couldn't refuse her. It wasn't in him to make a woman unhappy if he could help it. "Fine, but you owe me." He followed her back to the table. He'd expected some shit comment from Marc, but the bouncers were talking to him.

"Adrian, get the next berry." Desiree's smile was wide but there was a slight tension around her eyes as she glanced over his shoulder.

He followed her gaze. Ethan was on the balustrade watching them. He tipped his head at the other man and then plucked another berry from their plant. "Don't worry, I'm going to make this one count."

"I'm sure you'll try." Ellie smiled sweetly up at him.

"I'll do more than try." He dipped the berry in the green dye and then aimed, pretending to focus on Mistletoe Mary but actually paying attention to Ellie. She didn't disappoint him. Right as he was ready to throw, she dug her finger into his side. He caught her hand. "You want to hold hands. Aren't you a sweetheart?"

"Ah…that's okay." She tugged, trying to free herself from his grasp. "You should let go, so you can throw better."

"I have a feeling this will improve my aim." He tightened his grip on her hand, keeping it clasped to his side and then threw the berry. It hit the doll's upper thigh.

The crowd cheered.

"I can do better," he shouted as he grabbed his next berry, soaking it with green dye and then throwing it before Ellie could wiggle any more. He hit the doll on her stomach right at the bikini line. "Almost there." He glanced at Ellie and his grin slipped away.

She was pale, the red of her lips the only color on her

face. His traitorous heart flipped, filling his gut with guilt. "You don't have to do this," he whispered as he leaned down, pretending to kiss her ear.

"I'm fine." Her eyes darted to her ex who was watching them with a smirk on his face.

"Forget about him. He's not worth it." He was going to kick that guy's ass.

"I can't. Please just throw the berry and let's get this over with."

Ouch. That was not something he'd ever heard from a woman's mouth before and he never wanted to hear it again. He dipped the last berry in the liquid. Ellie stood like a statue by his side. He took careful aim and threw, the berry landing right on the doll's neck.

Ellie's head snapped toward his, a question in her big brown eyes.

He shrugged. He hadn't been trying to make her suspicious, but it was better than sad. His mission for the evening had changed from getting her into his bed, which he still wouldn't turn down, to making her forget her ex and smile, really smile, like she'd done when she'd been talking on the phone.

CHAPTER 9: ELLIE

Why had Adrian hit the doll's neck? Ellie's eyes narrowed at his slight grin. The man had to be up to something. All men were. All the time.

"Ellie, come over by me." Desiree stood between Mistletoe Mary and the last prop which was still covered by a sheet.

"Why?" She didn't move.

"For the game." Desiree smiled at her like she was a simpleton.

"Go on." Adrian nudged her with his elbow. "I promise not to bite, unless you want me to."

A sizzle of heat rushed to her face and other places, making her hurry across the stage before Adrian noticed. She didn't need him getting the wrong impression, which was actually the right one, but she'd go to her grave before letting him know that.

"Poor Mistletoe Mary," said Desiree. "She gets hit with berries and stained with dye but she receives none of the pleasure." She turned toward Ellie, yanking the sheet off the prop. "That's all for you."

Ellie's mouth dropped open. The large contraption looked a lot like what held up the doll. Two poles were affixed into wooden slats and secured by a rail at the top. Garland had been twisted over the top bar and the poles had been covered in gold and silver wrapping paper. Even the restraints hooked to the top and bottom of each pole were a festive red.

"Stand here"—Desiree motioned to the spot in the center of the device—"and give me your hands."

"Move on to the next couple," yelled Marc. "She's never going to go through with it."

Ellie's face paled but her back stiffened as she took that final step, turned and spread her arms.

"Grab the poles and hold on." Desiree smiled at her as she took one of Ellie's hands and put it around a pole.

"Use the cuffs." Ellie glared at Marc. The asshole looked so smug. She refused to back out of doing any part of this. She didn't care if Adrian fucked her right here in front of everyone. Her body froze. All the heat and desire from earlier and even her anger fled with her panic. Okay, she did care but she'd do it to prove Marc wrong.

"Are you okay?" whispered Desiree. "You don't have to do this."

"I want to." She forced a smile, glaring defiantly at Marc.

"Okay." Desiree affixed a cuff around Ellie's wrist. "You can stop anytime. Just let me or Adrian know. He won't force you. I swear, he's a good guy." She moved on to Ellie's other hand.

"There is no such thing." They were all like Marc who was counting the minutes until she backed out so he could insult her even more. Well, he could count forever because tonight she was going to show him that she was adventurous and sexy, and he'd thrown it all away.

"Feet?" Desiree looked at her.

She closed her eyes for one second, gathering her courage. She was already helpless but with her legs spread she'd feel so much more vulnerable.

"Are you sure you want to do this?" asked Desiree quietly. "I can make up an excuse or have the bouncers remove that friend of yours."

"He's not my friend." He'd never been her friend. He'd been her lover and then basically just someone who lived at her home, spent her money and made messes for her to clean up—kind of like a horrible pet. A bubble of nervous laughter rolled up her throat and escaped. "I'm sure. My feet. Tie my feet too."

"Okay." Desiree bent and the crowd cheered as she spread Ellie's legs and hooked them into the restraints. She straightened. "Adrian, time to collect your kisses."

CHAPTER 10: ADRIAN

Adrian's dick was about ready to burst through his pants. Ellie's lush body was restrained and open for him. Too bad they weren't in a playroom. It wasn't his style to fuck for the crowd but tonight he might make an exception.

Desiree stepped aside, calling him over.

He moved slowly toward Ellie, savoring the sight. Her chest heaved and her dress pulled tight against her large breasts. His eyes skimmed downward. It'd been a short, sexy dress before but now it was almost indecent. It'd slid so far up her legs that he was sure he'd see her panties when he knelt in front of her for his kisses.

He pulled at his pants, wanting to grab his dick and give it a few tugs. He needed something, anything to alleviate some of the tension it was feeling.

"Your hand is going to be all you get tonight," yelled her fuckwad of an ex-boyfriend.

He stopped, turning toward the jerk. "Shut the fuck up." He was done asking.

"Me?" Marc tried to look innocent, but his eyes were

hard.

"Yeah. You." He'd faced many enemies over the years and the body could lie but the eyes told all.

"It's a free country. I can say whatever I want."

"Not around me." He took a step toward the other man. "I'm not going to stand here and let you insult a lady."

"Lady?" Marc slapped the guy next to him. "She's as much of a lady as…"

A large hand landed on Marc's shoulder. Damon, the bouncer, pressed down making Marc's face pale. "I don't know if Bruce went over the rules with you, but you need to shut the fuck up or leave."

"Why? I'm not doing anything." Marc jerked free.

Adrian wasn't sure if he wanted to smile because the fuckhead was in trouble or growl because he'd wanted to be the one who wiped that smirk off the asshole's face.

"Adrian." Desiree touched his arm. "Let's get back to the game."

He nodded as Bruce, one of the few members of the Club he didn't like, was talking to Marc and calming the dickwad down.

"Adrian," Desiree spoke into the microphone this time. "It's time to collect your kisses."

One good note, his erection had cooled. He might be able to wait until they were in a back room before he fucked Ellie. He turned and that idea evaporated like sweat in the desert. His dick rose again at the sight of his lush goddess spread out like a feast for him. He could spend hours worshiping her, pleasuring her like this.

"Remember," said Desiree. "You can only kiss the places on Ellie that match where your berries stained Mistletoe Mary."

"I'd like to give her some stains," yelled someone from the crowd.

His gaze darted to the doll to remind himself of where he could kiss. He shouldn't have wasted the one on her neck. He could've made her smile after he made her come.

He moved toward her as if pulled by a string, his eyes locked on her breasts. Fuck, she had nice tits–large and soft. He could smell her—perfume, soft and flowery, warmed by her flesh. He wanted to see her ass. He'd bet it'd be displayed, just a bit, from the position of that dress. He stepped closer. "Can I touch her anywhere?" He was definitely going to grab that ass if he were allowed. His eyes darted to Ellie's and his dick deflated. Her face was pinched like it'd been when he'd first seen her but this time her soft eyes were wide with panic.

CHAPTER 11: ELLIE

Ellie tried not to yank on her restraints as Adrian strode toward her. She was helpless. Tied up and at the mercy of a stranger. Her heart raced. She should stop this. Shout to Desiree that she was done. She wanted to go home. Maybe the bouncer had made Marc leave. Her eyes darted over Adrian's shoulder. The bouncer was walking through the crowd and Marc was moving back toward the stage. Her chance was gone. If she didn't stay Marc would win.

Adrian stopped directly in front of her, his large body blocking her view of the crowd. "Can I touch her anywhere?"

Her breath caught and her eyes locked with his.

"Yes," said Desiree. "As long as Ellie is okay with it."

"Are you?" He lifted his hand, holding it near her cheek—close enough for her to feel his warmth but not touching her.

"Ah…" She didn't want him to touch her. He was a stranger, and she was on stage, but she also didn't want to back down. "Sure." She lowered her gaze. It'd all be over soon. He'd kiss her and maul her and then she'd smirk at Marc and go home to shower.

"Thank you."

Her eyes lifted to his. She hadn't expected that. Men like him never expressed gratitude when things went their way.

"Relax." His fingers traced her cheek like she was made of the finest porcelain.

"Kiss her," shouted someone.

"My pleasure."

She swallowed and his gaze darkened as he watched her throat.

"Can I kiss in any order or do I have to go in the same order as my berries?"

She wished he'd look at Desiree or something besides her because she couldn't pull her eyes from his. His dark green gaze tied her to him more firmly than the restraints secured her to the poles.

"Any order but only those five locations," said Desiree.

"Shame." He ran his thumb over her lower lip. "I should've aimed here."

His touch was soft but there was a promise in the heat of his gaze that made her panic drift away like wisps of smoke on a windy day. She could feel herself drawn to him, drowning in his eyes.

"I guess I'll have to settle for here." He brushed her hair aside and leaned closer, his face lowering to her neck.

She shivered as his hot breath caressed her skin.

His lips close to her ear, he whispered, "Do you want me to stop? I can say it's me. That I got a phone call or something like that."

The heat and tension cooled. He didn't want her. Marc was right; it was her. She bit the inside of her mouth to keep her sob from escaping. She was tied up like an ancient offering and this guy didn't want her. "Sure, if that's what you want."

He grabbed her chin, turning her toward him. "What do you want?" His eyes searched hers and she felt like he was flinging open doors that'd been closed for years and pulling everything out.

It terrified her. She had no idea what he might find or what he might reveal to her about herself. "I…I don't care. If you don't want to do this. It's fine with me." It wasn't. She hadn't wanted this but now she did. She wanted his lips on her–here on this stage in front of Marc and everyone.

"Are you sure?" His fingers tightened on her chin to the point of pain for one second before he eased up. "And before you answer, know that what I want is to devour you." His eyes bore into hers and she shivered from the heat. This wasn't desire. This was lust, rut, passion so desperate it'd burn. "I want to kiss every fucking inch of you until you forget everything but me." His voice was rough, like sandpaper on her skin.

"Kiss me," she whispered.

A growl tore from his throat as his hands dropped to

her waist and his mouth to her neck. His kiss was hot and wet. He didn't go slow but poured open mouthed kisses down her throat, nipping and licking, making her shudder. His large hands slid to her ass, pulling her against him. She moaned at the feel of his erection, rubbing along her thigh. His fingers slipped under her dress, squeezing her ass.

The crowd roared or at least she thought it was the crowd, but she wasn't sure. It might've been her blood pounding in her veins as Adrian's face lifted, his hot breath cooling her wet flesh.

"Now, for berry number one." His fingers drifted along the cleavage of her left breast. His eyes locked with hers as they slipped under the cloth. "May I?"

"Yes." It was the only answer she had. She could refuse him nothing with his fingers caressing her flesh and her nipples hard and eager for his touch. She didn't want his kiss on her clothes. She wanted it on her skin.

He slid her dress down, exposing her black lacy bra. "Beautiful." He bent, his lips and tongue teasing along the lace as he kissed her breast while his fingers rolled her nipple.

Her head dropped backward, and she moaned, arching her back and thrusting her breast more fully into his face. His hand was on her thigh, rough and strong, squeezing. Her legs pulled at the restraints, trying to get closer to him, to wrap around his waist and feel that long dick between her thighs where it belonged.

His mouth trailed across her chest to her other breast, moving closer and closer to her nipple. She arched more, eager for him to take her in his mouth.

"He's cheating," shouted someone on stage. "He's not kissing just where the berries landed."

Adrian raised his head and glared at the other contestant. "Why the fuck do you care?"

The guy shrugged, his eyes dark as his gaze skimmed down Ellie, making her want to hide behind Adrian. "I want my turn."

"Your turn?" Her words came out as a squeak. No. One stranger kissing her was enough.

"And you can have your turn—"

"What?"

Adrian glanced at her, frowning and shaking his head before focusing on the other guy again. "With *your* partner when I'm done." He dropped to his knees. "I still have two more berries."

Ellie's panic from the thought of everyone on stage kissing her turned to raging lust at the sight of Adrian on kneeling before her. Her body gushed with anticipation and she prayed it wasn't running down her thighs because that would be too fricking embarrassing.

CHAPTER 12: ADRIAN

Adrian knelt before Ellie, his dick pressing against his zipper. She was lush perfection—her thighs soft and round spread open for him. If they were alone, he'd fuck her right now. Unfortunately, it was apparent that this whole scene was new to her and she didn't seem like an exhibitionist. He could show her how fun that could be but not their first time.

"Berry number three…four if you count the miss." His eyes locked with hers as he lowered his face between her thighs. The scent of her arousal teased him, making his dick grow painfully hard. His hands shook as he grabbed her butt. He had to touch her and if it wasn't that lush ass, he'd be fingering her. Too bad she wasn't ready to do something like that in front of everyone.

His mouth grazed her thigh and she trembled. Her flesh was warm and perfumed with some kind of womanly soap and arousal. He had to taste her. He dragged his mouth along her leg, licking and kissing. She arched toward him, a soft moan slipping from her lips. He groaned as his mouth moved toward her pussy. No one would blame him for kissing her there. It was what they all wanted—a show.

"No cheating," chided Desiree. "You'll have to save kisses for other places until later."

"Fuck," he said against her thigh and then it hit him. "I'm not cheating. I'm moving to berry number five." He continued kissing his way up her thigh with hot, open mouthed kisses.

"What do you think?" Desiree asked the crowd. "Is that fair?"

"Hell yes!" shouted someone.

Adrian grinned at the eager agreement from the crowd. Sex is what they wanted to see and do. He had no problem putting on a show, but he wouldn't go too far, not without Ellie's consent. He glanced up at her and his blood thickened. Her brown eyes were lost to lust as she stared at him like a starving woman. Her luscious lips were parted, and her breasts heaved. She wanted his mouth on her as much as he did but until they were alone, it'd be through the underwear. He didn't want her regretting anything that happened between them tonight.

He kept his gaze locked with hers as he moved his hands from her ass. He lifted her dress, exposing her black lace panties. His eyes dipped down, taking her in before meeting hers again. "You're fucking beautiful."

Her eyes sparked as his breath teased her succulent flesh. He'd make her come right here with just a kiss and a touch. She was so sensitive and eager. He lowered his face, breathing her in, his dick protesting its confinement. He brushed his mouth against her pussy, and she trembled.

"Someone get some hot water because his face is going to stick to that frozen pussy. She has ice for blood," yelled Marc.

Adrian stopped at Ellie's gasp. He forced his eyes away from his treat and rage replaced the desire in his blood. She stared out at the crowd, her face pale and tight and then she lowered her gaze, meeting his for one second before looking away, a blush covering her cheeks.

He didn't say a word. He never did when he was this angry, but he moved—faster than anyone anticipated. In two seconds, he was on his feet and flying off the stage at that asshole. He was going to shove his fist down the jerk's throat and pull out his nuts.

He hit the floor and charged. Marc was surprised but his face took on a calm expression and his stance widened. The guy knew how to fight. Good. So did he but before he could reach his opponent four of the Club's bouncers moved between them.

"Get out of my way." Nothing was going to keep him from beating the shit out of this guy.

"Can't do that," said Damon.

"He's a dick."

"Let's take this outside," said Marc who was trying to get past the bouncers. It seemed he wanted the fight as much as Adrian.

"That's not going to happen." The crowd cleared as Ethan sauntered toward them. "Adrian, you know the rules." His eyes landed on Marc and then on his friend Bruce who stood to the side. "Bruce, is this your guest?"

"Yeah, but he didn't start it. Adrian did. He came after—"

"Shut up, Bruce." Ethan turned back toward Adrian. "There's no fighting inside or outside the Club. Ever. Period."

Adrian straightened and nodded. He knew the rules. He had his reasons for breaking them and he wasn't sorry, but rules were rules. "I understand." He'd take his punishment like a good Marine. "Sorry, sir."

CHAPTER 13: ELLIE

Ellie struggled in her restraints as Adrian launched himself off the stage at Marc. "Stop!"

He didn't listen. Men like him never did but the big jerk was going to get the shit kicked out of him. Marc was a mixed martial arts instructor. The man was an ass, but he knew how to fight.

"Desiree, please! Get me out of here."

But the other woman was busy yelling for bouncers who were already moving quickly through the crowd. She prayed they'd get there before Adrian got hurt.

"Hold still." The contestant who'd been eager for his turn began unfastening her.

She sighed as the bouncers stopped the fight. "Thank God." She straightened her clothing.

"Don't be too thankful," muttered Desiree. "Ethan's not happy. Fighting isn't allowed. Ever."

She rubbed her wrist as she stepped toward the other woman. "What will he do?"

"Probably kick Adrian out of the Club."

"But…it wasn't his fault. Not really. Marc started it."

Desiree shrugged. "Marc was being a jerk, but he didn't start the fight."

No, Marc's abuse was more mental. It had been for years, but she just hadn't realized it. She wasn't going to let Adrian take the blame for this, not without trying to help him. She headed across the stage.

"Wait. Where are you going?" Desiree waved and a bouncer stepped in front of the stairs.

"To help Adrian."

"Not without your gift."

"My what?"

Desiree grabbed the Santa bag and held it open in front of Ellie. "Everyone who plays gets a present."

"A…I don't want one." She glanced back at Adrian. He did not look happy.

"You'll both enjoy it. I promise." Desiree grinned mischievously.

"Fine." She grabbed a package from the bag. "May I go now?"

"Of course." Desiree pulled a chip from the bag before putting it down. "The fight is over. Time to play. The next couple is Yellow."

The bouncer stepped aside, and Ellie hurried through the crowd. "Wait, please." She stopped at Adrian's side. "Please, don't kick him out. This is my fault."

"Your fault?" Ethan's eyes landed on her.

"Yes." She straightened so she didn't melt into a puddle of mush. This guy was even better looking up close with his dark blue eyes and the face of a Nordic god.

"How is this your fault? From where I stood, it looked like you were tied up on stage"—his gaze wandered slowly down her frame, stopping on her stomach or at least she was going to call it her stomach—"ready to be worshipped. You, my dear, should be the most upset." He took a step closer. "To be denied pleasure at that moment." He frowned, shaking his head. "It's criminal."

"Ah…I…" What was wrong with her? He was right. She'd been ready, eager for a stranger's lips on her and in front of everyone. That was so not her.

"Pleasure? She never comes," said Marc.

Ellie's face heated as all eyes fell on her. Marc wasn't exactly lying. She'd had issues recently, but she was overworked, and Marc did nothing around the house. Still, sex with her couldn't have been great for him. He prided himself on his prowess and she wasn't a good actor.

"I could fuck her for hours and nothing," continued Marc. "Not a tremble. Bitch can't even fake it right."

"That would be your fault not hers," snapped Ethan as Adrian lunged forward but the bouncers tightened their grip on his arms, keeping him in place.

"Ignore him." She stepped in front of Adrian. She didn't want him to get hurt. "He's not worth it."

Adrian's eyes dropped to hers and she wanted to cry. There was no desire in his gaze or even humor. She'd even be fine with anger, but instead his green eyes were filled with pity.

"Adrian, your membership is rescinded until

February," said Ethan. "Get out of here and see the lady home."

The bouncers dropped their hold on Adrian but stayed close.

"Come on." He took her arm.

She nodded and let him lead her toward the exit.

"Have fun with your blue balls and your hand because they're better than that cold pussy any day," shouted Marc.

There were a couple of snickers from the crowd and Adrian's hand tightened on her arm.

"Keep going," said one of the bouncers. "Ethan will take care of this."

The unfairness of it all swept through her like a fire. Marc had cheated on her. He was the asshole, but she was the one getting the looks of pity and amusement. She was not letting Marc win. She'd already been humiliated. There was nothing left to lose. "One moment, please." She smiled up at the bouncer as she shoved the gift into Adrian's hand. "Hold this."

"What is it?"

"A gift from Desiree for playing the game." She started to walk away.

"Ellie, let's go." He tugged on her arm.

"In a minute." She yanked free from his grasp and strode back through the crowd. She and her sister had their mother's temperament. They were generally easy going, passive even, letting the men in their lives take the lead until it went too far, and Marc had gone too far.

The bouncers still held Marc between them. His lip

was now busted open and Ethan wiped blood off his knuckles with a napkin.

"I thought there was no fighting." She gave Ethan a disgusted look.

"It wasn't a fight. I slipped." Ethan didn't smile but his eyes sparkled. "Fortunately for me, he caught me before I fell."

"With his face?"

"Apparently." Ethan smirked.

"Thank you." Another charming, sexy, alpha caveman. This place was crawling with them. She stopped in front of Marc who cocked his eyebrow as if challenging her.

"I am not cold. Maybe if you could last more than three minutes, I would've been a little more eager for sex." That was kind of a lie. Sex between them had been good at the beginning.

"My dick wasn't made for the freezer. When they make parka condoms, I'll give you another go."

"I am not cold. I love sex just not with you."

"Right. Didn't your other boyfriends cheat on you too?"

Tears filled her eyes. She'd told him that in confidence and he was airing it out for everyone.

"But keep telling yourself that I'm the problem if it makes you feel better."

"I am not cold." She could say that until she grew old, but no one would believe her. She wasn't sure if she believed it herself. Marc was winning. His words would haunt her forever unless... "I just need a real man. I should have no trouble finding one here."

She turned, sauntering through the crowd. Her ass was too big. Too many days sitting behind the desk and on the couch at home, but men seemed to love it, so she let her hips sway with each step. She headed straight for Adrian who'd moved closer, the bouncers still at his side.

He watched her, his expression unreadable. She prayed he'd go along with this. He'd wanted her earlier. Hopefully, he still did. She stopped in front of him. "And here's the man I want." She grabbed his tie, pulling him down until their lips were almost touching. "I'm going to fuck you until you can't move and then I'm going to suck you off until you beg me to stop."

She threw a glance over her shoulder at her ex. Marc was pissed. She'd finally won a few points. As her and Marc's relationship had deteriorated, she'd stopped giving him blowjobs and she was really good at them. Now, she had to follow through with this because alpha a-holes talked and bragged. Marc would hear if she went home alone and she refused to let him win.

CHAPTER 14: ADRIAN

Adrian let Ellie pull him through the Club by his tie, grinning at the nods from some of the other patrons. He didn't mind being led around like a stud because that's what he was tonight. She was angry and upset and she needed to feel in power. He was the perfect guy for her.

Having grown up the only boy of seven children, he had no problems taking orders from females. In the bedroom he was usually dominant but tonight—his eyes fell on her lush ass—he'd make an exception.

If she needed to take the lead and ride him hard, who was he to object? He'd wanted to make her happy since the moment he'd seen her. He was one lucky SOB that she'd decided sex would make her happy. It'd certainly give him a Merry Christmas.

They stepped outside and her pace faltered. He couldn't let her lose her steam and start having second thoughts about the rest of their night.

"My car is to the right. The blue Mustang."

"Figures."

"What does…" Nope. He wasn't going to argue with her. She didn't seem the type who'd get more turned on by it and he wasn't losing his shot at getting laid. "Unless you want to drive. That's fine with me. Whatever you want. You're in charge."

She gave him a suspicious look.

"I mean it. Seriously."

"You swear?" She let go of his tie.

"Absolutely." It might kill him, but he'd let her be in charge, until he couldn't.

"You drive. I took an Uber here." She headed for his car. "Too bad I left my keys at home. Marc probably drove my car. I'd love to take it and leave the bastard stranded."

"I could hotwire it for you."

"Really?"

"Yep." He'd do it too. It was her car so he wouldn't be stealing it.

"How would you open the door to get to the console?"

"I don't have a slim jim, so I'd have to break the window."

"No." She looked horrified. "Absolutely not."

"Okay. My car it is." He was pretty sure he'd made some points for the offer.

He followed her, clicking his key fob and unlocking the door. He started to grab the handle, but she beat him to it, opening the door and sliding into the passenger seat.

He hurried to the driver's side, tossed the present between them and started the car. "Your place or mine?" Damn it. That'd been a stupid question. Her ex probably had a key or lived with her. He had to keep his head in the game before he screwed up his night.

"Yours." She stared out the windshield her face tight.

He wasn't sure if she were nervous, hurt or angry but he did know that look on her face meant no sex. He had to get her mind on something else. Something hot. The Mistletoe Game. She'd been creaming her panties when he'd been sucking her thigh. "Why don't you open our gift?"

"What? Oh." She stared down at the package as he pulled onto the main road.

"Let's see what we won." He turned on the radio, finding something upbeat. He needed her in a good mood.

"Sure. Why not."

It wasn't the enthusiasm he was looking for, but it was a start, and he knew Desiree. This gift would be fun and kinky.

Ellie tugged on the ribbon, opening it slowly.

So, she was one of those people who took her time with a gift, savoring the pleasure to come. He could work with that. He'd unwrap her the same way—slowly with kisses and touches. He shifted, giving his pants a little tug to make room for his swelling cock. Luckily, his place wasn't far away.

She carefully tore the paper where it was taped.

"You saving that?" He couldn't help it. She was so adorable, opening that gift like she was performing surgery. He was more of a tear-into-it kind of guy.

"Why? Do you want it?"

"Me? No. Why would I want old wrapping paper?" His laughter died at the look on her face.

"It's stupid. I know." Her finger traced the paper where it was still attached to the box.

"It's not stupid." Shit, she'd been serious. It was time to scramble. He'd lost some major ground. "But I wouldn't be able to use it again. I have no talent for wrapping gifts. I always pay some group of kids to do it at the store."

"Thanks, but it's still stu—"

"It's not stupid. Nothing you think or feel is stupid." He was going to beat the snot out of her boyfr…her ex-boyfriend.

"Thanks." Her face softened or maybe it was an illusion from the streetlight as they passed. "Okay, it's silly then. Wrapping paper isn't expensive."

"But it isn't about the money, is it?" He didn't think money was an issue for her. She held herself and dressed like a woman who had money.

"No." Her voice quieted to almost a whisper. "I just…It seems a shame to use it once and throw it away."

"It is. You should keep it."

"I can't keep all the wrapping paper I get."

"You get that many gifts? Do you have rooms full of used wrapping paper?"

"No." She laughed.

His heart thudded and his dick stiffened at the sound. It was a true laugh. She held nothing back and it was the sexiest thing he'd ever heard. There was a throaty resonance to it that made his blood roar. He had to make this woman laugh again and again. He wouldn't even need her to touch him. All he'd need was that sound for his dick to stand at attention.

"Then"—he reached out, placing his hand over hers on the package—"you can keep this piece." He gave her hand a squeeze before letting go. She hesitated so he added, "You can keep it to remember tonight." Damn. Now, he kind of wanted it as a keepsake.

"Tonight?" She turned toward him, placing the half-opened present between them. "You mean the night my boy…ex-boyfriend humiliated me in front of a room full of strangers?"

Fuck. He'd stepped in it this time. He'd kind of forgotten about that but he wasn't a novice at easing women out of a snit. He would've never survived childhood without those skills. "I don't see it that way. I see tonight as the time you made a stand. The night you dumped a loser who didn't deserve you. The night you showed everyone that you were a woman who went after what she wanted." He smirked. "Me."

Her jaw dropped for a second. "You are even more arrogant than I thought."

"That's nothing. Wait until you get to know me better." He was making progress. Her tone had been filled with humor.

She laughed. "Unapologetic too. Wow, I sure know how to pick them."

"You obviously have discriminating tastes." His grinned widened. This was the mood he needed.

Lighthearted bantering and teasing equaled mental foreplay. "As do I." He let his gaze skim across her body for one hot second. "And trust me; you taste exquisite."

CHAPTER 15: ELLIE

"Oh…uh." Ellie had no idea what to say to that. Adrian was so freaking hot and funny and…a stranger. She never went home with strangers. Even in college she'd been a "girlfriend-boyfriend" kind of girl.

A lot of her friends had hooked up, but not her. Of course, most of her friends were now happily married. Some already had kids and here she was twenty-six and alone again.

Adrian pulled into an apartment complex and parked. They were here. He got out of the car. She couldn't just sit here, but she didn't move. She didn't do things like this. She dated and then had sex. She didn't pick up men in bars. She also didn't let herself be tide spread eagle in front of a crowd of people while a stranger kissed her body. The memory of Adrian kneeling before her made her blood turn thick and hot. Maybe it was time for her to change. Her usual way of doing things had gotten her nothing but heartache.

Adrian opened the door. "Are you coming?" He leaned

down, his green eyes concerned. "Would you rather I took you home?"

"Home?" She rolled her eyes. "Where I'm going to run into Marc?" The bastard would slither into the apartment and shower to wash away the scent of perfume. Then he'd slip into their bed like nothing was wrong, as if he hadn't just wasted years of her life. It was definitely time she changed her habits and the type of guy she dated. "No, thanks." She got out of the car.

Adrian was exactly her type–hot, arrogant, alpha all the way–but this wasn't a date. This was the first step toward her new life, and she was going to use him to help her get there.

She grabbed his tie again. She'd loved pulling this alpha male along behind her like her puppy. Her eyes darted down his body. She'd rather lead him around by his dick, but she wasn't quite ready to be arrested for public indecency. "Let's go finish our game."

"That's an excellent idea." Adrian followed behind her like a good boy as she marched across the parking lot.

Tonight, she was going to take what she wanted from this man. She was filled with frustration and pain and anger and she was going to fuck him until she couldn't think. She stopped at the front of the building. She had no idea where he lived.

"Need something?"

Her spine bristled at the smugness in his tone. He'd have that damn sexy, know-it-all smirk but she was going to change that. She spun around, pulling on his tie until he bent toward her. "I need you inside me. All of you. Every delicious inch of you." Her hand dropped, caressing him through his pants. His dick grew under her fingers. He was not a small man. Her body melted at the thought of how he'd feel filling her, stretching her. "But if you keep being an ass, I may go home to my vibrator."

"Like hell you will." His mouth landed on hers as he lifted her, pulling her tight against his strong body.

This man wasn't playing. His lips devoured hers, his tongue invading and commanding. She softened against him, allowing him to lead where they both wanted to go.

"Wrap your legs around my waist." He started around the corner.

She obeyed, needing to feel him there, rubbing against her but she was in charge. "No." She let her legs drop back down to the ground.

"No?" His step faltered but he continued walking toward the stairs.

"I give the orders. Not you," she said against his lips before kissing him, her tongue diving into his mouth.

He grabbed her head, holding her for his exploration and taking control. She sucked on his tongue and it was like opening the flood gates. He groaned, pushing her against the brick wall and grabbing her leg, pulling it to his waist. She moaned as he rocked against her, rubbing her pussy with his hardness and heat.

His lips trailed to her neck and then her ear, nipping her slightly. "Either I'm going to fuck you right here or you're going to wrap your legs around my waist. We need to get up the stairs and into my apartment but I'm not putting you down. Nothing is getting between us, not even air." His fingers slid under her dress and between her legs. He pushed her underwear aside, stroking her wetness. "You're so fucking ready for my dick. Please, wrap your legs around me."

She gasped as he slid a long finger inside her, his thumb caressing her clit. She should say no. She should take control, but her body needed this, needed him and he had said please.

CHAPTER 16: ADRIAN

Adrian was going to explode in his pants and humiliate himself if he didn't get inside of Ellie soon. He groaned as her legs finally wrapped around his waist. "Thank you," he muttered against her skin and then hurried up the stairs, taking two at a time. His heart thudded so hard she had to be able to feel it and his cock grew as it rubbed against her pussy with each step.

This time was going to be fast. He fucking prayed she'd enjoy it. If not, he'd have to work all that much harder to get back inside her because he was going to fuck her more than once tonight. The way she tasted and melted against him made him want to fuck her until he passed out or his balls shriveled up like dried plums.

He stopped at his door, pushing Ellie against the wall and holding her there with his body as he dug in his pants for his keys.

She trailed kisses across his face and down his neck. "When we get inside, I'm in charge."

Her hot breath tickled his ear, making his balls tighten.

"Next time." He slid his key in the lock and stepped into his apartment, kicking the door closed behind him.

"No. Now." Her legs dropped from around his waist, but he caught them in mid-fall, his hands cupping her ass and pulling her back against his aching flesh.

"Fuck, Ellie. I need you now." He stumbled toward his bedroom as she struggled to lower her legs.

"Let me go." She nipped his ear. "Or we stop."

"Fuck." He almost shouted. This was unfair. It wasn't that she didn't want it because she definitely did. She just wanted to be in charge and that was bullshit, but it didn't matter. He was a gentleman. Even with a raging hard-on the man let the woman decide. It fucking sucked but he dropped his hold, letting her slide down his body.

She stepped away, her face flushed and her lips red from his kisses. His chest heaved, his eyes on her disheveled dress. Her cleavage was almost spilling from the neckline and the short dress still rode high on her hips.

"Widen your legs." His gazed raked over her pretty black panties. He needed to see how wet he'd made her.

"I give the orders." She touched his chin, raising his eyes to hers. "Take off your clothes."

His teeth ground together but he yanked his shirt from his pants. He loosened his tie and pulled it over his head as he shrugged out of his jacket. He unbuttoned a couple of buttons and then pulled his shirt over his head. His hands went to his belt and his dick rose as her eyes followed his movement.

"Wait." She stepped closer. "I'll do the rest."

CHAPTER 17: ELLIE

Ellie couldn't believe she was being this bold, but she loved it. She'd undressed Marc but it had always been on his orders, but not tonight. This time, she was the one in charge.

She stepped closer until her breasts brushed against Adrian's chest with each breath. Her nipples tingled at the contact. She placed her hands on his abdomen. He was like hot, marble–solid, smooth but so warm. Her eyes met his as she ran her hands upward.

Adrian's jaw was tight. She could almost hear his teeth grinding. Poor man was barely keeping it together. How far could she go before his control snapped? Her hands drifted down his chest and skimmed along his abdomen. His muscles twitched as she unbuckled his belt, letting her fingers slip beneath the waistband of his pants.

"Hurry up." His voice was gruff with need and it made her insides melt.

Her body was so ready for him to fuck her, but she didn't want this to end. "Order me again and I'll go slower." She smirked up at him as she pulled his belt slowly from his pants.

He grabbed her chin. She braced for his dominance, for him to explain how this worked and how he was in charge.

"You go slower, and I won't be any good to either of us." His thumb skimmed over her lips. "I need you, Ellie. I can't hold out much longer." His green eyes were almost black, like a forest at midnight. "I swear. I'll let you do whatever you want next time but right now...I can't wait."

She hadn't expected him to negotiate. "Tonight."

"What?"

"I'm in charge the rest of tonight." She unbuttoned his pants and unzipped them. His erection strained at the fabric and she gave it a squeeze.

"Fine. Okay. Whatever you want as long as I can have you now."

She wanted him too. She needed him, needed a cock sliding hot and hard inside her. "Then I'm all yours."

CHAPTER 18: ADRIAN

As soon as Ellie agreed, Adrian moved. It wasn't even a conscious thought, his body just reacted. He wrapped his arms around her because he had to feel her against him again, surrounding him. His lips found hers and he lost himself in her heat and wetness. He stumbled forward as she clung to him, her kisses as desperate as his.

The bedroom was too far away. He lowered her to the couch, his lips everywhere–her mouth, her neck, the warm scented skin above her breasts.

Her hands tangled in his hair, holding his face to her breasts. He could die like this, smothered by skin softer than warm satin. He pushed the dress and bra out of his way, he had to see her nipples, taste her.

He paused for one hot second as he stared at the dusky rose perfection below him. Her chest was flushed with excitement, the color almost matching the heat in her cheeks. His eyes locked with her brown ones, soft and wide with desire, as he lowered his face slowly toward her nipple. Her mouth opened on a whisper of a gasp as he took her between his lips and sucked. Her back arched and he pulled more of that succulent flesh into this mouth.

His pushed her dress up and slid his hand between her legs, stroking her. She was wet and hot and so fucking slick. So ready for him. "Now, Ellie. Please. I need you now."

"Yes."

She was like an angel singing the best song in the world—consent to fuck. He shoved his pants down, freeing his cock.

"Condom," she said.

He pulled her underwear aside and positioned himself at her entrance. She was so fucking hot and wet. He rubbed the tip of his dick along her folds, coating himself with her desire.

"Condom." She yanked on his hair. "Adrian, get a condom."

"What? Oh. Right." How the fuck had he forgotten that? Even at the Club he still wore protection. As the third child of seven, he knew that mistakes happened, and he wasn't taking the chance of an unwanted pregnancy. He yanked up his pants from around his ankles and pulled out his wallet. He grabbed the condom and tore it open, sliding it over his cock. "Now, where were we?"

He kissed her. It started softly. She'd lost some of her desperation. He needed her to want him as badly as he wanted her because he wasn't going to set any records for duration this time. He reached between her legs as he devoured her lips, loving the taste of her. His thumb teased her clit, swirling and pressing down until she writhed beneath him, her hips rotating. Fuck, he had to know how that felt with his dick buried inside her.

He grabbed his cock, shoving her legs farther apart and positioning himself at her entrance. Her heat soaked through the latex of the condom as he thrust into her. His chest swelled with pride as her gasp turned into a moan.

CHAPTER 19: ELLIE

Ellie's eyes closed in ecstasy as Adrian pushed inside her, stretching her. It felt wonderful. A low moan escaped her throat. God, she'd missed sex like this–desperate and hot.

"Look at me." Adrian's breath tickled her cheek.

She forced her eyes open. He stared down at her, a superior smirk on his handsome face. It should be illegal to be this good looking and not be locked away in some Hollywood mansion. His body thrust rhythmically, hitting all the right places. She stifled her moan, digging her fingers into his arms. Okay. Fine. Right now, he had a right to be cocky.

"Like that, do you?"

But not that cocky. He was already was way too attractive. She didn't need to feed his ego. "It's okay."

"Okay?" His smirk slipped away, and his eyes narrowed. "Judging by that moan, you think it's better than okay."

"Moan? I didn't moan." She feigned innocence.

"Liar and I'll prove it."

She bit her lip to keep from moaning again as he pulled all the way out and pushed inside her slowly, making her feel every inch. Her pussy clenched around him, encouraging him to move faster, push harder. He ignored her body and continued his slow assault. She closed her eyes, looking at that gorgeous face was too much, and clamped her mouth shut, stifling her moans. He was arrogant enough; she wasn't going to let him know what he was doing to her.

When his dick was buried balls deep inside her he stopped moving. "Look at me."

She forced her eyes open.

"Stop biting your lip." He kissed her quickly, nipping her mouth. "That's my job." He shifted his hips, retreating from her body.

She tugged on her lip with her teeth to keep from protesting, but his mouth landed on hers.

"Oh, no you don't. I want to hear that moan." His lips brushed hers with each word.

"I didn't moan."

"Liar. Tell the truth or you'll be sorry." The tip of his cock slid inside her and he thrust hard, pushing all the way in.

"Fine." She rolled her eyes, trying to cover her desire, but her word came out low and throaty.

He grinned with triumph, increasing his pace, fucking her in long, strong strokes.

"But I didn't lie. It wasn't a moan you heard. I was

trying not to yawn."

"What?" He stopped his slow assault on her body, his dick halfway inside her.

"Sorry." She wasn't one bit. Men like him needed their ego deflated. Her pussy clenched around his cock, as long as this didn't deflate with it. "You wanted the truth."

"Ha. You are such a little liar." He grinned. "I'm going to enjoy making you admit that you're lying."

"I'd admit it if I were, but I'm not." She smiled back at him in challenge.

"You're going to eat those words, sugar." His mouth dropped to her breast.

She wrapped her hands in his hair and arched her back as he suckled her, sending electricity from her nipple to her pussy. She pulled him closer, needing to feel more. He tugged her nipple between his teeth, and she throbbed in anticipation of the pain-pleasure that was coming her way.

She barely noticed that he'd bent her legs at the knees and had shifted his position as his cock slid in and out at a steady pace, keeping her body dancing on the edge of release.

"Last warning," he mumbled against her breast.

"Huh?" She had no idea what he was talking about or why he was talking instead of sucking her nipple.

"I'll assume that means you aren't willing to tell the truth yet."

"Truth?" Her mind scrambled. "Oh. Right. No, I'm about to yawn again though so could you get a move on."

He chuckled against the side of her breast, sending

vibrations through her. "Don't say I didn't warn you."

The next second his mouth was hot on her nipple, teasing and biting, making her squirm. She wasn't sure if she were trying to get closer or away. The pain-pleasure sparked a fire inside her. He pulled out and slammed into her, hard and fast at an upward angle that was…incredible. He shifted again, thrusting inside her and this time she couldn't hold back the gasp as he hit her G-spot.

"What was that?" He thrust harder and faster, hitting that spot over and over. "I didn't hear you."

Her mouth opened as her body bucked under him, trying to rub that lovely cock even harder against that spot. His hands held her ass, shifting her so that the next thrust slammed full force against her G-spot. She gasped for air because he'd just taken everything from her and then he was back, doing it again and again. Her fingers dug into his back. Part of her wanted to pull him closer, climb inside his gorgeous body while another part wanted to push him away. The sensations were too much, too fast but he didn't stop or even slow down. Instead he fucked her faster, his breath coming in pants as his fingers dug into the soft flesh of her ass, holding her in place as he ravaged her body.

"Look at me." His other hand grabbed her hair, yanking her head backward.

Her eyelids fluttered open. His face was hard with passion, no teasing in his green eyes for almost the first time tonight. He pumped into her, his dick hitting that spot over and over, his gaze never leaving hers. He thrust again shifting his hips and hitting her G-spot so hard that she couldn't stop the scream as she came, clinging to him with every inch of her body.

CHAPTER 20: ADRIAN

Adrian tried not to come. He wanted to fuck Ellie straight into another orgasm, but her body was squeezing his dick so tight, so perfectly, that there was no way he was going to last. He thrust into her one last time and exploded, his body tightening with his release and then he dropped onto her, boneless and spent. He'd be happy staying like that, but he was a big guy. She couldn't be comfortable with his two hundred pounds lying on top of her. He rolled to the side, pulling her with him and wrapping her leg over his hip.

She sighed softly, her eyes closed. Her cheeks were flushed a rosy pink that drifted down her chest, getting fainter with each inch. Her hair was mussed, tumbling around her face. She was the most beautiful thing he'd ever seen. He'd known she was pretty when she'd smiled but he'd never imagined how lovely she'd be when satiated.

He brushed his fingers over her cheek. "You still with me, babe or did you pass out from pleasure?"

"What?" She opened her eyes.

"Oh, good. You're back." He grinned. He loved teasing her. She was so prickly.

"I wasn't gone."

"You sure? I think you blacked out after you screamed."

"I did not scream."

"You are such a liar." He chuckled. "I made you scream. Loud. So loud that I wouldn't be surprised if one of my neighbors called the cops." He lifted a little, glancing at the door.

"It wasn't that loud." She slapped his shoulder.

"So, you admit I made you scream?" He dropped back onto the couch.

"You make me want to scream right now." Her brow raised in challenge. "You are the most arrogant man I've ever met."

"For good reason. I have many talents. You can vouch for that." His hand skimmed over her thigh. Her skin was so soft, he could run his hand across it all night.

"You're fast. I'll vouch for that." She pulled her leg down and sat up. "You were in such a hurry we're still dressed." She began straightening her clothes.

"Didn't stop you from coming hard." Yes, it'd been a fast fuck, but she'd enjoyed it so much she'd screamed. She should be thanking him or at least clinging to him in exhausted bliss.

"You're unbelievable."

"Thank you. It was great for me too." He kicked off his shoes and pants. "Next time, we'll be naked, and it'll be even better."

"Next time?" She stood. "Sorry but this was a one and done for me and now, I've gotta go."

"Wait." He stood, enjoying the way her eyes lingered on his chest for a few minutes. She wasn't as immune to him as she pretended. He moved closer. He was so not done fucking her yet. "Stay. It's early. We'll rest and then fuck again. I promise to go slower. As slow as you want." He cupped her cheek. "Stay the night. You're the best present I'm going to get this year."

"Charm won't work on me." She moved his hand away from her face.

"What will?" He was willing to do anything to keep her here naked in his bed.

"Your obedience." She smiled.

CHAPTER 21: ELLIE

Ellie fought a grin as Adrian's face fell. Men like him—alpha jerk-faces who called all women babe, sugar or some other meaningless endearment—never allowed anyone else to be in control, especially not a female. "You decide. You let me be in charge and I'll stay." She ran her hand down his bare chest. Lord have mercy, this man had a great body and the face to go with it.

Her other lovers hadn't been unattractive; they just hadn't been this dreamy. She probably hated that most about Adrian. Any guy who looked like he did would stray and she was done with cheating men.

The look on his face was worth a million dollars. He'd probably never had a woman turn him down, especially not after fabulous sex. "And if I don't, you'll leave?"

"Yes." She skimmed her nail around his nipple.

"How about, I'll try." He ran his hands down her arms, stirring her blood.

"Not good enough." She flicked his nipple, and his eyes darkened.

"It's the best I can do."

"Then I go." She'd get a hotel for a few hours and then go to her parents' house for Christmas.

"Come on." He moved closer. "Let's negotiate."

"Nope." She forced herself not to lean into his warmth. Confidence and cocky arrogance were her weaknesses. She needed to change that.

"Okay. Let's go to bed. I'll let you be in charge."

"You will?" She didn't trust him.

"Yes, until I can't anymore."

"That's not good enough." She rested her hands on his chest. She didn't want to leave but she was done letting men like him win.

"Would you rather I lied to you? Promised you something I may not be able to do?"

"No." She hadn't expected him to be so frank about this. Marc would've either lost his temper or pouted.

"I promise, I'll do my best to let you be in charge. I swear." He crossed his finger over his heart. "I'll do whatever you tell me."

"Starting now."

"Absolutely." He grabbed her waist and pulled her closer. "Let's get you out of these clothes and go to bed before we end up fucking on the couch again."

She melted against him. He was already growing hard and it was so nice being with a man who wanted her. "Okay."

He unzipped her dress and she stepped away from him, letting it slide down her body.

"But we're going to bed to sleep."

CHAPTER 22: ADRIAN

Adrian couldn't take his eyes from Ellie's breasts. The pretty, black bra showcased her nipples more than concealing them. Her panties were the same color, high on her waist and almost see through. These clothes were made for a man—to drive him crazy with lust and indecision. He wanted to tear the lingerie off her and yet, he wanted to leave it on because they were so fucking hot.

"Did you hear me?" Her tone was slightly amused.

"What? Yeah." He took her hand. "Let's go to bed."

"To sleep."

He dragged her toward his bedroom. "Sure. Later. Sleep." Right now, he was going to fuck her until she screamed again.

"No." She tugged on her hand, stopping him. "We're going to get in your bed and sleep now."

"But…" He glanced down at his erection.

"We may even snuggle." Her chin pointed in the air.

"Snuggle? I do *not* snuggle."

"I'm in charge, right?"

"Fuck." He was an idiot.

"We'll do that later. If you behave." She strode past him, her hips swaying seductively, and he followed, his dick leading the way.

CHAPTER 23: ELLIE

Ellie stopped at the foot of Adrian's bed, loving the way he trailed after her. "Get in."

He frowned but did as he was told and flopped on the bed. She waited until his eyes met hers before unhooking her bra. She held it up for a minute, slowly letting it drop. Her breasts swayed as they came free, her nipples hard and ready for his mouth.

"Turn around. I want to see your ass."

She started to turn but stopped. "I'm in charge." She walked to the other side of the bed and crawled in pulling up the covers.

"What are you doing?" He rolled toward her. "You want me to take off your panties? I'd be happy to help."

"I think I should leave them on."

He smirked. "Okay but you know they won't stop me." He pulled her close, his dick hard and ready. He rocked his hips, rubbing his cock against her ass.

She wanted to push back, to open her legs and let him inside her. He'd feel even bigger from behind but then he'd be in charge. "Oh no, we're not starting that." She moved his hands from around her waist and scooted across the bed.

"I thought you wanted to snuggle."

"That was not snuggling."

"It could be later when we're done." His voice was thick and warm, tempting like hot chocolate syrup.

"No. For now, you sleep over there"—she scooted farther across the bed—"and I'll sleep over here." Luckily for her, she was a come once-a-night kid of gal. She'd never been able recharge and come again. She needed at least four or more hours before her next orgasm.

"You know we'll both sleep better if we come." His voice was a purr and a promise.

"According to you, I came so hard I almost passed out."

"You did."

"If you say so."

"I don't just say so. You did." The sexy gruffness in his voice had been replaced by irritation.

"Then I must be exhausted. Worn out from my orgasm." She forced herself to stop grinning and plastered the most innocent expression she could on her face as she shifted so she could see him over her shoulder. "I guess you're too fabulous for your own good."

"Don't tell me you're not horny." He leaned up on his arm, smiling as her eyes drifted down his chest.

Man, he had one hot body. She was starting to feel desire pooling in her belly and lower, but she had to ignore it. If they fooled around now, she'd be disappointed. She needed to sleep but her body was second guessing her mind. It kept believing his eyes with their promise of more exquisite pleasure. "No. I'm good."

"You are that and together we're terrific." His eyes were hot on her body, igniting heat wherever they touched. "Come here, babe."

That endearment cooled her blood like she'd jumped into a snowbank. "I'm in charge and I say we sleep."

"Okay. You're in charge. Give me an order. I'll go down on you. I'm very good at that too."

She struggled not to shiver. Marc had not liked doing that for her and she really, really missed it but she had to be strong. "Later. I'm tired."

"You are such a fucking liar."

"Good night." She rolled over, smiling as he grumbled something about bossy little liars before punching his pillow and rolling away from her.

CHAPTER 24: ADRIAN

Adrian woke, his senses on alert. He'd heard something—a quiet sound like someone trying not to wake him. Ellie moaned softly in her sleep. His body relaxed. They were safe. No one was trying to break into his apartment. Her legs moved and she moaned again. She must be having a bad dream. He rolled over to shake her shoulder when a movement under the covers caught his attention. She sighed, the sound coinciding with the fluttering of the blanket.

What the hell? He sat up, turning on the lamp by his bed and angling the light away so only a soft glow filled the room. Ellie was on her back, sound asleep but her face was flushed, and her mouth slightly opened. She moaned again and her legs shifted.

She was dreaming about sex and he was damn sure going to watch. He yanked the covers off her, revealing her lush breasts with nipples already hard and ready for his mouth. Her hands grasped at the mattress and then at the side of her leg, her hips wiggling. He wanted to feel that motion as she rode his cock, but he didn't move. Not yet. Her hand drifted across her thigh. Was she going to touch herself while he watched? He scooted closer. Her fingers fluttered on the top of her leg but didn't move between them. She moaned again but this time it was a sound of frustration not of pleasure. His little liar had gone to sleep as horny as he'd been and now, she was suffering.

He edged closer and her face turned toward him, eyes still closed. He ran his hand across her thigh. "Do you want me to help you out?"

She sighed softly and her leg shifted toward him, opening herself for his touch.

"I'll take that as a yes." His hand teased along her inner thigh. Her breathing increased, making her gorgeous breasts lift and fall just for him. Her nipples looked painfully hard. He should soothe them for her. He leaned down blowing softly on one turgid peak. "Do you want me to kiss you here?" He ran his tongue over the hard, little nub while his fingers danced between her legs, coming close to her center but not touching.

Her hands tangled in his hair, pulling him toward her chest.

"Another yes." His lips attached to her nipple, sucking gently as his fingers slid her underwear aside and slipped between her folds.

CHAPTER 25: ELLIE

Ellie was having the best dream. Marc was making love to her, like he used to. She buried her hands in his thick hair. It was longer than before and so soft. She spread her legs for his touch and his fingers slipped inside her.

She moaned as he found a spot that sent sparks flying through her blood. This was heaven. He moved downward taking his talented mouth away from her breast. She tightened her grip in his hair, trying to keep him right where he was.

"Ouch." He chuckled. "Don't worry, babe, I'll be back." His hand moved from between her legs and she clamped them shut, trying to keep him touching her. He laughed again, kissing her softly. "Trust me. I'm not going away for long." He pried her fingers from his head before removing her underwear.

She'd forgotten she'd still had them on, but they were gone now. She reached for him but stopped as he kissed his way down her body, leaving hot, wet kisses on her sensitive flesh. He nipped her hip as his large hands grabbed her legs spreading them.

Oh, he was going to...Marc never did this but...She groaned as his tongue teased along her folds before flicking her clit. Her eyes popped open. This wasn't Marc. She looked down.

"Merry Christmas." Adrian gave her a cocky grin before his fingers tightened on her thighs and his mouth covered her pussy.

"I...oh...oh." She gasped, her body tensing as his magical tongue teased her clit.

"I hope you don't mind." He shoved two fingers inside her, stretching her. "You were having a kinky dream, but you seemed frustrated. I thought I should help."

Her hips reached for his touch. He sucked her clit as his fingers danced along her G-spot, sending shocks of pleasure shooting through her body.

He lifted his head and stilled those fingers. "But if you want me to stop..."

"Don't. Please. Don't stop." She was pretty sure she'd cry if he did. She was almost there. She grabbed his head and pushed him back between her legs.

"Merry Christmas to me." He yanked a pillow from his side of the bed and shoved it under her hips, making her pussy an offering for his mouth.

CHAPTER 26: ADRIAN

Fuck, Ellie was sweet and so fucking responsive. Adrian slid another finger inside her as he teased her clit with his tongue. His other hand tightened on her thigh, keeping it in place as she tried to vise grip his head. He stroked her faster and faster. He was going to make her come and then he was going to fuck her right off that cliff again. He'd make her scream so loud she lost her voice.

"Oh...god...please....I can't." Her hands clasped his head, trying to push him away one second and pull him closer the next.

He bit down gently on her clit and she screamed, her hips thrusting against his face. He sucked her clit, his fingers still working frantically inside her, wringing every last bit of her orgasm from her body until she collapsed, boneless on the bed.

He sat up, wiping his face before propping one hand on each side of her head. "Now, you're going to come again."

Her face was flushed, and her eyes slowly opened. "I can't." She touched his cheek. "But you go ahead." She ran her foot along his calf.

"Oh, no. I'm not doing this alone." He leaned on his one hand while his other grabbed a condom from the nightstand.

"Of course not." She kissed him. "It's not you or anything. It's physically impossible for me to come again so soon. I need some down time."

"Not when you're with me." He winked at her. "I insist."

"You insist?" She didn't seem amused or like she believed him, but he'd show her.

"Yep." He rubbed his dick along her wet, hot slit.

"You're unbelievable. Trust me. I've tried to have more than one orgasm, but I just can't. So, don't tell me...."

She gasped as he slid inside her and his dick grew even harder. That surprised sound of pleasure-pain was the best aphrodisiac in the world. If a woman didn't gasp when a man entered her, he should zip up and go home.

"Trust me, little liar. I'm gonna make you come so hard on my cock that you will black out this time." He put all his weight on his arms as his hips thrust slowly in and out of her wet heat. She felt fucking perfect...hot and soft and slippery, her body squeezing his dick. It almost made him come right then, but this wasn't going to be a fast wham-bam like earlier. No, this time he'd fuck her slowly, enjoying every moment.

CHAPTER 27: ELLIE

Ellie felt boneless from her orgasm but that certainly wasn't the case for Adrian. He was hot and throbbing inside her and annoying her to no end. She wanted him to finish. The nerve of him thinking he knew her body better than she did. This man was more arrogant than anyone she'd ever met, and she knew some cavemen.

"Look at me." He grabbed her chin, turning her head toward his. His face was hard with passion and his eyes gleamed as he pulled almost all the way out and thrust back inside her—again and again, in no hurry, just rocking into her over and over like a wave on the ocean. "You're so fucking gorgeous." His mouth lowered to hers and his kiss was sweet and slow.

She wrapped her arms around his back, running her hands along all that smooth, warm flesh, loving how his muscles moved with each thrust. His lips trailed across her cheek and down her neck, while he kept fucking her in that slow and steady rhythm. She should be relaxing into the feeling but instead of soothing her, her body was starting to respond. It wouldn't last. She'd heat up a bit, but she wouldn't be able to come again. She never did. She had tense, wild orgasms but only one. She needed a few hours to recharge before she could climax again.

"You feel so fucking good." His voice was a coarse whisper in her ear. "But I know you can feel even better. Tighter. Hotter." He kissed her neck hard, pulling the flesh into his mouth and sucking before laving it with his tongue.

She gasped as he lifted one of her legs and plunged into her hard and fast, going deeper in this position.

"There we go. You like that." His pace increased as he leaned up, his dark green eyes locking with hers.

She wanted to deny it. She couldn't really be spiraling toward another orgasm, but his thrusts came hard and fast, giving her no time to catch her breath. Each stroke was like gas on a fire and her body heated, turning to liquid.

"That's it." He closed his eyes for a minute, his jaw clenching. "Fuck. Yes."

The sound of flesh hitting flesh filled the room, but she barely heard anything over the roaring of her blood. Her other leg wrapped around his waist and she dug her nails into his ass. She was so close. Her breath came in pants as he fucked her furiously. She clung to him, trying to keep his hard cock inside her but he was stronger than she was. His dick retreated before slamming back inside her again and again. She writhed under him, needing him closer. Needing him to stay, hot and hard, inside her. Her hips bucked and she screamed as she came. He grunted, thrusting into her one more time, his entire body stiffening like a statue as he groaned his release.

CHAPTER 28: ELLIE

Ellie woke, stretching. She felt great but a little sore. It was definitely a good kind of sore. A great sex kind of sore. Her eyes popped open. She didn't remember falling asleep. The last thing she remembered was Adrian's large body draped over hers after the best orgasm she'd ever had. She'd actually come twice. Lord help her, there'd be no dealing with the man's ego now.

She rolled over and glanced around the room. She was alone. She scooted toward his side of the bed and buried her face in his pillow. Damn, he smelled as good as he looked. She inhaled deeply before rolling back to her side of the bed. She could not let him catch her doing that. He was arrogant enough.

"Good morning. I like how you smell too." Adrian's deep, sexy voice made her jump.

This was so embarrassing. How much had he seen? Hopefully, not everything. "I wasn't...I was looking for a clock."

"With you face buried in my pillow?" He laughed.

"You are such a liar."

"No, I'm not." She held the covers to her chest and sat up. "I was looking…" She lost her train of thought or maybe her ability to think.

Adrian leaned against the bedroom door frame. He had on a pair of loose, gray sweats that hung low on his lean hips. He wore nothing else, no shoes, socks or more importantly shirt. His chest was just as sexy as she'd remembered. Large and muscular with a light sprinkling of hair that trailed downward where a large bulge formed in his once loose pants.

"Keep looking at me like that and you're going to make me late to my parents' house." He sauntered to the bed and leaned down.

She fell back, trying her best to keep from making contact. If he touched her, she'd probably grab him and ride him like a bronco. He followed her to the mattress, bracing one arm on each side of her. She was trapped and she loved it. His beautiful green eyes locked with hers until they closed as he kissed her softly. She melted at the tenderness and then incinerated as he pulled down the blanket, planting a hot, wet kiss on each of her breasts, right next to her nipples. One of her hands stroked his arm while the other skimmed through his hair, telling him in no uncertain terms to stay right where he was.

"These are too tempting to resist." He pulled a nipple into his mouth, causing her body to arch toward him like she was his puppet. He smiled up at her, his hot breath tickling her wet and sensitive bud. "And you're gorgeous enough that I think my mom would understand me being late for Christmas."

"What?" Shit. Damn. It was Christmas.

"Don't worry. I won't tell her the real reason." His grin widened and then slipped away as his mouth lowered to her nipple, sucking.

For one second her hand tightened in his hair, pulling him closer. She wanted this man. The tug on her breast was making her pussy tight and needy but it was Christmas. She had to get to her parents' house. He moved to the other nipple, his fingers playing with the abandoned one.

She sighed, her legs drifting open for him. Maybe they had time. The room was still mostly dark; only a bit of light crept through the drapes. "What time is it?" She pulled his head closer.

He trailed kisses down her chest, pushing the covers out of his way. Oh, sweet Jesus, he was going to go down on her again. Desire pooled between her legs.

"Adrian." She ran her fingers up and down his arms, loving the feel of those strong biceps. "What time is it?"

"Time to fuck." He grabbed her hand, placing it on his dick.

She squeezed, helping him to grow with her touch as his hand slipped between her legs.

"No, what time is it really? I have to be at my parents' house at one." Her legs spread for him, giving him all the access that he needed as she slid her hand inside his sweats and grabbed his cock.

"Please tell me they live close by. Really close." His

thumb teased her clit.

"No, they live about an hour away from my place and I have to go home first." She pulled her hands from his pants. "What time is it?"

He flopped over her, landing on his side of the bed. "I was afraid you were going to say that. It's almost noon."

"What?" She jumped from the bed. "I'm going to be late. I've got to go. Where are my clothes?"

"On the chair." He sat up, watching her with an amused expression on his face.

"Damn it. I never sleep this late." She yanked on her dress, not even bothering with her underwear and bra. "I have to go home, shower—"

"You can shower here." His eyes roamed up and down her body.

"Like that'll save time."

He shrugged. "We can make it quick. I take superfast showers."

"I don't have time for a quickie."

He hopped from the bed. "It's a perfect solution. You need to shower, and you don't want to spend Christmas at your parents' all tense with sexual desire."

"I'll survive." She grabbed her shoes and slid them on. "Purse?"

"Living room by the couch." He followed her out of the bedroom.

"Great. Thanks." She pulled her phone from her purse and headed for the door.

"What? No kiss goodbye?"

She paused. She was being kind of rude. "It was fun. Thanks."

"Ouch." He put his hand over his heart.

"Please." She laughed as she stepped out the door, pressing a button on her phone. "Mom. Yeah. No. Everything's fine." She may as well tell her now. "Ah...actually, Marc and I broke up." She walked down the stairs. "No. I'm fine. I'm just running late." She glanced at her phone. "I should be there around two. I'll try and get there earlier but...let's plan on two. Okay. Love you. See you then." She hung up and stopped in the parking lot. She didn't have her car.

"Need a lift." Adrian grinned down at her from the balcony.

"Ah...yeah. Thanks." She ran her hands over her arms. It was cold outside.

He headed down the stairs, carrying a gym bag. His hair was wet, and he wore jeans and a T-shirt with a hoodie.

"You showered and changed already?"

"I told you I took quick showers." He pressed his key fob, unlocking the doors before popping the trunk and dropping his gym bag inside.

"Did you use soap?" She got into the car.

"Of course." He slid into the driver's side. "I even cleaned all my naughty parts." He glanced at her as he started the car. "You're welcome to check if you want. Next time, I'll let you do the cleaning. It'll be a lot more fun that way, but the shower will take a little longer."

"I hope so. Speed Racer isn't my type."

"You had no complaints last night."

"Like I said, it was fun."

"Fun?" He frowned at her. "I think it was more than fun for both of us." He stopped the car at the entrance to the apartment complex. "Where to?"

She gave him directions to her apartment, and he pulled onto the main road.

"Admit it. It was better than fun." He glanced at her.

"Okay. It was fine." She winced. Fine was not a word a man wanted to hear about his performance in bed. "Look, I'm sorry. I'm just not looking forward to being late for Christmas and explaining about Marc but that's not your fault." Mom would have a hundred questions and she'd feel like a loser again with another failed relationship. "Last night was fun and the sex was great but that's all it was. Sex."

"Okay." He looked at her like she'd freaked out for no reason, which she had.

"Oh, god. Now, I'm embarrassed." She was acting like he wanted more than praise for his performance. "With the way you were going on, I thought that you wanted to see me...Slow down. That's my apartment up there."

"I know." He frowned. "That's why I have the turn signal on."

"Oh. Right."

He pulled into the parking lot of her apartment and stopped the car.

"Thank you for the ride and for last night." She leaned

over and kissed him softly. "It was exactly what I needed."
She got out of the car and so did he. "What are you doing?"

"I'm going to walk you to your door."

"That's not necessary." The entrance to her building
was only a few feet away.

"It is with your ex still hanging around. I doubt he
moved out last night."

CHAPTER 29: ADRIAN

Adrian was not letting Ellie go to her apartment alone with that ape of a boyfriend there. The guy had been itching for a fight last night and he wouldn't be in a better mood today, especially since Ellie had stayed out all night. If she were his woman, he'd want to kill the guy who'd taken her home.

"No, I'm sure he hasn't moved yet, but I'll be fine. I'm not afraid of Marc," said Ellie.

"I don't care. I'm going to escort you to your apartment and stay until you leave for your parents' house." He moved over to her side. "Don't give me that look."

"What look?"

"That you're so sweet but you're an idiot look."

She laughed. "Sorry but—"

"I don't want to hear any excuses. I've seen that look from my sisters too many times to count and I'm almost always right and they were the idiots."

"Almost, but not always."

"Enough to know, I know best." He swore sparks shot

from her eyes. He had no idea how those words had come out of his mouth. He knew better than to say that to a woman, but his brain didn't work around her, probably because most of his blood was surging to his cock.

"I'll be fine." She turned and headed toward the building, dismissing him.

He followed. He didn't take orders from her, especially when he did know best.

She stopped, her eyes narrowing at him for a second and then her face softened. "I appreciate the gesture, but do you really think you coming upstairs with me is going to make things better with Marc?"

"It'll keep you safe and that's all that matters." Plus, he might get an early Christmas present and get to kick the shit out of the guy.

"He won't hit me. That's not his style."

"Good. I'm glad I don't have to kill him but he doesn't need to talk to you like he did last night either."

Her face heated. "Yes, you're right but you coming upstairs will make it worse. Plus, he's probably not even home." She stood on tiptoe and kissed his cheek. "I'll be fine. I promise."

He could follow her and piss her off even more, but she truly didn't seem worried about her ex. She'd been more concerned about being late to see her parents. He pulled his phone from his pocket. "What's your number?"

"Why do you want my number?"

He gritted his teeth. Usually after a night with him the women *wanted* him to call them. "So, I can text you and make sure everything is all right."

"That's not necessary."

"It is if you want to go up there without me." He crossed his arms over his chest. "I'm not budging on this. Those are your options."

Her eyes narrowed and her lips thinned. He was pretty sure she was searching for a weakness, but she wouldn't find one. He was a master at battling women.

"Fine." She gave him her number and he put it into his phone.

He texted her and her phone beeped.

"You're testing me?" She stared at him incredulously.

"You've lied to me before."

"I did not lie."

"Not this time."

"Not last time either." She walked toward her building.

"You didn't answer my question."

She stopped, looking at him over her shoulder. "What question?"

He waved his phone at her.

She glanced down at her message. "Why do you need to know my apartment number?"

"If you don't answer my text, I'm coming up. I mean it."

"Oh, my god." She texted him the number. "I'll be fine. Marc isn't violent."

"Men do crazy things when their women stay out all night."

"I'm not his *woman*. He cheated on me, remember?

He's moved on."

"Just because he cheated doesn't mean he wanted to break up and he's definitely not going to like knowing you've already found someone else."

"That's exactly why you can't come upstairs with me. He'll never know for sure what happened last night after we left the club as long as you stay here." She gave him that superior look common to all women when they thought they'd won an argument.

"He'll know."

"Because I didn't come home? I could've stayed at a hotel. Alone. Or maybe I went to my friend Alison's house." That look became even more smug.

"That hickey on your neck tells a different story." He braced himself for the attack. Once they got out of junior high, females didn't like being branded like that—ever. He usually didn't do it because of that but with Ellie he'd wanted that asshole to know she was his. Hell, he wouldn't mind everyone knowing.

CHAPTER 30: ELLIE

"A hickey!" Ellie touched her neck. "Why would you...I can't believe...Arghh." She needed to leave now, or she was going to wipe that smug look off his handsome face with her fingernails. She spun around and hurried toward her building.

"Don't forget to text me," he called after her.

It was childish but she waved her middle finger at him over her shoulder. His laughter made her walk faster. She was going to kill him if she had to spend one more minute with him. She flung open the door and headed across the foyer. He was the most arrogant, brutish man she'd ever met, and she'd dated her share of alpha a-holes. A hickey? This day couldn't get worse.

She caught the elevator and jabbed her finger onto the button for the third floor. A hickey? What was he a teenager? She snorted. His maturity was probably pre-teen. She got off on her floor, unlocked her door and went straight to the bathroom. Right now, she didn't even care if Marc were there.

She lifted her hair and peered into the mirror. Yep, there it was in all its blue-bruised glory. A hickey. How was she going to hide the damn thing from her family? It wasn't exactly tiny. She searched the rest of her neck. He'd spent a lot of time there. Her body flushed at the memory. "No. You're not going to get turned on by that. He was….is a jerk. An asshole." Her phone beeped.

ADRIAN: Everything okay?
ELLIE: Besides the hickey, yes. Asshole.
ADRIAN: Is he there?

She hadn't seen Marc in the kitchen or living room.

ELLIE: I don't think so.
ADRIAN: Think? Make sure.
ELLIE: UR not my boss.

But she left the bathroom and walked to the bedroom, peeking inside. The bed was made. Marc hadn't bothered to come home. It was fine with her. She never wanted to see him again anyway.

ELLIE: He's not here. Go away.

She waited, expecting some smartass reply but the phone didn't beep. Good. He was a jerk anyway, but he had been nice to her last night. Her face flushed. The sex had been fantastic but that was all it was. That was all she was going to let it be.

From today forward she was done with hickey-leaving Neanderthals. She'd find herself a nice, quiet accountant or someone like that. A guy who had very little testosterone instead of these cavemen she always dated. Even her first boyfriend had been a macho jerk. He'd been her next-door neighbor…Shit. She didn't have time to daydream. She had to go. She hurried into the bathroom. She still had to shower, change and drive to her parents' house. Her hand froze on the shower nozzle. Marc had her car.

CHAPTER 31: ADRIAN

Adrian stared at his phone. Well, that text was rude, but he'd forgive her. Ellie had been kind of pissed about the hickey. Plus, he definitely wanted another round in the sack with her. He was looking forward to making her admit that he was the best fuck she'd ever had. She sure had been his—the way she clung to him and surrendered. Even her take charge attitude had turned him on. He'd never thought to play the Bottom, but it might be fun once in a while with her as Top.

His phone rang. "Hey Mom, Merry Christmas. Yeah, I'll be on my way in a few minutes."

Ellie raced from the apartment running in the opposite direction from him.

"I need to call you back." He hung up the phone and ran after her. He glanced to the side, expecting her hulking ex to be barreling down on them but the area was quiet. "Ellie, wait!"

She didn't even pause. He'd kill Marc if that bastard had touched her. Damn it. He should've listened to his gut and gone upstairs with her. She hurried around the side of the building and he picked up his pace. He almost slammed into her as he raced around the corner. Only his instincts kept him from knocking her down. Instead he pivoted and smashed into the brick wall.

"Where is he?" He'd deal with the pain in his shoulder later. He grabbed her, shoving her behind him.

"Stop it. What's the matter with you?" She tried to step around him, but he blocked her with his arm.

"Where is he?" He repeated, senses on alert for any movement or sound.

"Let go of me." She pushed his shoulder.

"Not until you tell me where Marc is." So, he could beat the shit out of the guy.

"I don't know." She shoved him again.

"He's not chasing you?" This time he let her step around him.

"What? No." She looked at him like he was crazy. "The only one chasing me is you." Her foot tapped on the pavement.

He recognized that sound. It was the pre-battle cry of all women. Any sane man would back away slowly but right now he wasn't sane. His blood pounded from thinking she'd been hurt. His fists itched to sink into Marc's face and torso but the only one here for his frustrated rage was her. "I wouldn't have been running if you hadn't come charging out of the apartment like someone was trying to kill you."

"Please. It wasn't that bad. I was just in a hurry." She

did manage to look a little ashamed.

"Not that bad?" He was going to shake some sense into her but instead he threw his hands up and spun around. He didn't trust himself to touch her right now. If he did he'd end up kissing her. That'd lead to a public fuck and they'd both end up in jail on Christmas. He was pretty sure neither his mother nor Ellie would be amused.

"Fine. I'm sorry that I scared you."

He glared at her. Scared wasn't the right word for the terror that'd race through him followed closely by the need to protect her.

"I...Marc isn't home. Didn't come home." She started walking back toward the door.

"That doesn't explain why you ran out of your apartment." He trudged after her. It looked like he was going to have to pry the information from her.

"I don't have a car."

"And you ran out of the building like it was on fire because of that?" He was going to throttle her, and no one would blame him.

"I was upset." She shot him a dirty look. "My day hasn't been going all that great."

He had to admit, that stung a bit. "If you'd stayed in bed another thirty minutes it would've at least started with a bang."

The look she gave him made it clear that she didn't find him the least bit amusing. "I'm already running late and it's Christmas. Then"—another dirty look—"I find out I have a hickey on my neck."

He couldn't help it, his chest puffed out a bit at that. It was a nice one—big and purple.

"And now, I don't have a car. I'm going to have to see if I can find an Uber who's working on Christmas or take a taxi which means I'll be even later. My mother isn't going to be happy with me."

"I can drive you."

She stopped and turned toward him. "You want to come to my parents' house for Christmas?"

Her tone told him that the correct answer was no which meant the only response he could give was…

"I can't stay long. I have to go to my parents' house but sure, I'd love to join you for an hour or so." It took every ounce of military training he had to not burst into laughter at the horrified look on her face.

CHAPTER 32: ELLIE

"You can't stay long?" Ellie's head was going to explode. Adrian had to be kidding. They'd just met.

"I really shouldn't but since you insist, I'll call my mom and tell her I'll be late."

She grabbed his arm when he started to pull his phone from his pocket. "Don't call your mother."

"I have to. I was talking to her when you raced out the door." He frowned. "Actually, I'm surprised she hasn't called me back yet. I told her I had to go and rescue the woman I'd picked up at the sex club and—"

"You did what?" Ellie was pretty sure glass shattered nearby from her screech.

"Oh, shit. You should see your face." The asshole burst out laughing.

"You are such a jerk." She shoved past him and headed for the door to her building.

"Ellie, wait." He caught up to her.

"It wasn't funny."

"It was. You'd think so if you could've seen your

face."

"Yeah. Right." She'd had all she could take today. This week. This freaking year.

"Hey. Come on. Don't be mad."

He ducked his head trying to see her face, but she walked faster. She wasn't going to let him see her cry.

"Come on. Don't be mad at me." He trailed along beside her like a giant, pesky mosquito—buzzing and annoying.

"Go away." She hurried into the building and to the elevator.

"I can't. Not if you're mad at me." He stopped at her side.

"I'm not mad. Now, go away." The elevator opened but he didn't move. "I swear, I'm not mad at you. Have a great life and a Merry Christmas."

He could go to his family and celebrate while she had to deal with no boyfriend, no car and trying to explain everything to her parents, including a hickey. She stepped inside, wiping at her eyes before she turned around. He walked into the elevator behind her.

"Why are you here?"

"I'm driving you to your parents' house." He glanced slyly at her as he hit the button for the third floor. "I can't wait to meet them."

That was it. Ellie's body actually shook with her rage and frustration. "This is all a big joke to you, isn't it? My breakup. Last night. My horrible life."

"No. I'm sor—"

115

"It sucks but it isn't funny." She jabbed his chest as he stood there his arms open and a look of panic on his handsome face. "*You* don't have to explain why you're coming home alone and late on Christmas." Tears rolled down her cheeks and his look of panic grew. She was pretty sure that if he could he'd burst through those doors like a cartoon character to get away from her. She should stop. This wasn't his fault, but the words kept coming. "You don't have to see the look of pity from your family because the man you thought you'd marry and have kids with is gone. Almost three years of my life gone. Wasted on a cheating, arrogant bastard."

The elevator slowed but she didn't. She was getting this all out and he was going to hear it. Not that any of it was his fault but he'd pushed her past her limit, and it was all coming out.

"And on top of all that they're going to want to know why I'm so late. I'll have to lie to them because I'm definitely not admitting that I was so upset last night that I grabbed the first guy I found and took him home. But let's not forget the hickey?" She pointed to her neck. "There's no way they won't see that. I can cover it today but I'm spending the night. Tell me." She poked his chest again. "How do I explain that without sounding like the biggest slut in the world?"

The elevator door opened, and he stood there staring at her like she was a train wreck. She didn't blame him. She was a complete and total wreck, but instead of him fleeing, she did. She tried to walk but her feet wouldn't obey, and she ran to her apartment.

CHAPTER 33: ADRIAN

Adrian watched as Ellie ran from the elevator. What in the hell had happened? He'd seen meltdowns before, but he'd never caused one. He hurried after her, slowing his pace when he was almost to her side. He'd learned from his sisters that sometimes men should be present but silent. Very, very silent. Even a sigh could set her off again.

She opened the door and stepped inside her apartment. He quietly let out his breath when she didn't slam the door in his face. He'd had his foot ready to stop it but thankfully he'd be able to walk without a limp for the rest of the day.

He followed her into her house but stopped as she continued down the hallway. He waited in the living room. It was a nice place. Neat. Homey with expensive furniture but it was older and comfortable looking.

She came back into the living room, her eyes red and puffy. "I'm sorry."

"No. I'm sorry." He walked toward her. If he'd ever seen someone who needed a hug, it was her.

"Stop. Please." She held up her hand and took a step

back. "Thank you for offering to drive me to my parents' house but I'll call a cab."

"Don't. I was kidding about meeting your parents. I'll drive you and drop you off. They won't even see me."

"You don't have to. I'm fine."

"I want to and it's on my way." She was as far from fine as he'd seen, but this time he kept his thoughts to himself.

"On your way? How do you know where my parents live?"

"I don't." He smiled sheepishly. "But you said it was an hour drive which means it's out of town. My parents live out of town. So, it's on my way."

"That makes no sense at all. Your parents may live in the opposite—"

"It doesn't matter." He started to reach for her but put his hands in his pockets instead. "I'll take you. I owe you."

"For what?"

This was a risk. She'd either be charmed or tear his head off. "The hickey." He winced, waiting for the blow but she only shook her head at him.

"My parents live in Glenfalls."

"Perfect." He'd live to see another day. "Like I said. On my way."

"Really?"

"Kind of. My parents' house is in Cedar Ridge."

"That's an hour out of your way."

"Nah. I'll take the back roads from your parents' house. It'll take about thirty minutes."

"Still. It's Christmas. It's too far. I can't ask you—"

"You didn't. I offered."

"You know, we're not going to have sex again."

"Whoa. Where did that come from?"

"If you think that doing this means we're going to have sex, it doesn't. I want that to be clear upfront."

"I didn't expect sex." But he didn't like how she said it like it'd never happen again. He hadn't planned to have sex right now or on the trip to her parents' house, but he did plan on fucking her again soon.

"Good." She eyed him warily. "You really don't mind?"

"Not having sex?" Damn it. He hadn't meant to say that out loud.

"No. Taking me to my parents' house."

"I don't. I swear."

"Thank you." She smiled slightly. "It'll just take me a minute to shower and change. I promise."

"No problem. I'll wait here." He tipped his head toward the couch.

"I'll hurry." She slipped back into the bedroom and the door lock clicked.

"Really? You locked the door? Now, I'm hurt." He smiled as he heard her soft laughter, wishing he could see her face. She was so fucking gorgeous when she smiled but there'd be other smiles. He'd make sure of that. He dropped onto the couch and pulled out his phone to call his mom and let her know he was okay, but he was going to be very late.

"Okay, all ready." Ellie walked into the living room about fifteen minutes later, carrying a small bag.

"Damn, that was almost as fast as my shower." He stood from the couch. "Did you use soap?"

"Of course." She rolled her eyes at him, but she was obviously in a better mood and she looked fabulous. She wore black slacks that hugged her hips and made his hand itch to spank that round, firm ass and a green and black sweater with a high collar that hid her hickey.

She walked into the kitchen and started rummaging through a drawer.

"Do you need me to carry anything down to the car?"

"Like what?" She glanced at him as she pulled out a paper and pen and moved to the table.

"Presents."

"No. I give everyone cash." She scribbled something on the paper.

"Cash?" His mother would skin his hide if he gave his sisters cash.

"Yeah. Don't make it sound like I'm giving everyone a turd for Christmas. Cash is king." She finished writing on the paper and put it on the refrigerator where it couldn't be missed.

"What's that?" If she were leaving a love letter to that asshole, he'd…He wasn't sure what he'd do because he was too much of a gentleman to leave her stranded here on Christmas, but he'd want to.

"A letter to Marc."

"Why?"

"To tell him to be out of the apartment before I get back. What did you think it was?" She gave him a curious look.

"I don't know." He still wasn't sure. She lied quite often.

"You can read it if...."

He didn't even let her finish before he was in front of the refrigerator. "Well, I'll be. The little liar tells the truth for once."

"I always tell the truth." She headed for the door.

"That's another lie." He followed close behind her, letting her feel his body next to hers and hopefully, reminding her of how good they'd felt together.

"I haven't lied. I speak only the truth." She glanced over her shoulder at him, a teasing glint in her big, brown eyes, as she walked out the door.

"Ha." He stepped aside so she could close and lock her door. "All you did was lie last night."

"I did not."

They started down the hall.

"I can't believe you're still afraid to admit that I'm the best fuck you've ever had."

"I'm not afraid. I just don't lie." She grinned. "It was nice though."

He laughed. "If that was nice, I can't wait to hear how you describe the next go-round."

She stopped at the elevator and looked up at him,

suddenly serious. "Adrian, I wasn't kidding about that."

"About what?" He pressed the button, not wanting to hear her answer.

"About sex. We're done. It's not you; it's—"

"It's me." He finished for her as the elevator door opened. "That's the biggest bullshit lie—"

"Please, don't be mad." She stepped into the elevator.

Mad? He wasn't mad. He was frustrated and determined but not mad because this wasn't over. He followed her inside and pressed the button for the ground floor.

"I just broke up with Marc and I don't think this is a good time to start seeing someone."

"But last night was?" He stared down at her, his brow lifting.

"I know. It was stupid. A mistake."

His teeth ground together. Okay, now he was getting mad. Last night had not been a mistake. The elevator opened and they stepped into the foyer and walked outside. He headed for his car but had only taken a few steps before he noticed she wasn't following. He turned.

"I should call a cab."

"Why the fuck would you do that?"

"Because I just told you that—"

"That you don't want to have sex. Fine. Whatever. You told me that upstairs too. So, what. I don't intend to try and fuck you in the car so you're good."

"That's not what I meant."

"Then you think I'm a big enough asshole to leave you

waiting on a cab on Christmas solely because you don't want to fuck me again?"

"Well…"

"I'm not that kind of guy." He continued to his car and opened the passenger door. "Now, get in and stop being a dumbass."

Her eyes narrowed at him, but she walked to the car, stopping at the door. "You're sure you don't mind."

"I don't mind taking you to your parents' house. I swear."

He took her bag from her and put it on the back seat as she slid into his car. He walked around the vehicle and got into the driver's side.

"Thank you again." She seemed so small and unsure of herself.

He didn't like that. He wanted the woman who'd dragged him out of the Club by his tie. "Consider it my Christmas present to you."

"Oh. Okay. Thanks."

"Don't mention it…again." He started the car and pulled out of the parking lot.

"Okay." Her hands fidgeted in her lap for a moment and then said, "If you don't give your family cash what do you give them?"

She was trying to lighten the mood. He wasn't thrilled about her *this is over* declaration, but he had an hour to change her mind and he wasn't going to do that pouting. He'd tried that tactic when he was a kid and his sisters had just teased him.

"Something that I think they'll like."

"Everyone likes cash." She laughed.

"Yeah, I suppose but my mom always made us get each other gifts that meant something. It didn't have to be big or expensive. Like this year I bought my second oldest sister, Deb, an ereader filled with books. She's married and has kids. I think she'll like that she can steal some time for herself while waiting in school lines or at doctor appointments."

"That's really sweet."

"Nah, just something I think she'll like." He usually kept this family stuff to himself, but he'd definitely scored a point.

"It's still sweet and it's a great Christmas gift."

"You know what else is a great Christmas gift." He glanced at her, trying to judge her mood.

"Yeah, cash."

"This is better than cash and it's free."

"Okay, I'll bite. What Christmas gift is better than cash and is free?"

"Sex." He kept his face serious as he glanced at her again. "In case you want to get me something. You know, because I'm sweet and thoughtful."

"And because you're giving me a ride to my parents' house?"

"I didn't say that." He wasn't that stupid.

"I am not paying for this ride with sex." She tried to sound annoyed but there was laughter in her voice.

"Of course not. The ride is free." This time he couldn't

stop the smile. "Just like both times last night but tipping is encouraged."

She laughed and he wanted to stop the car to enjoy that sight but there was traffic, so he only took a quick peek. She had the best smile he'd ever seen. It made her glow. It was almost as sexy as how she looked after she came. He could not go the rest of his life without seeing that sight again. He was going to do whatever he had to in order to get back between her legs and make her smile.

CHAPTER 34: ELLIE

"You have six sisters?" Ellie couldn't even imagine that. "Don't get me wrong, I love my sister and brother but four more of them would've made me crazy."

Adrian laughed. "It was rough sometimes, but it has its upside too." He turned on the blinker and pulled into a gas station.

She glanced at the clock on the car stereo. They'd been driving for a half hour. Time had flown by. She had to admit that he was fun to talk to. She was in a much better mood than she'd been in earlier today.

A text message beep sounded from her purse and her good mood vanished. She didn't even want to think about Marc right now. She glanced at her phone as she pulled her wallet from her purse. Her good mood returned. Alison had texted her, not Marc.

Adrian pulled up to the gas tanks and turned off the car before opening the door.

"Here's some money for gas." She held out a twenty.

"I got it."

"Please. It's the least I can do." Marc never balked at taking her money. Actually, he'd become accustomed to it.

"I don't need your money."

"I know you don't need it but—"

"I don't want it either."

"Please, take it." She was so used to paying for everything that she hadn't heeded the change in Adrian's tone. "You're going out of your way to—"

He grabbed her chin and leaned toward her."It's not your money I want."

"Ah…" Her eyes dropped to his lips. They were so close and so…kissable.

"I will never accept your money." His eyes dropped to her mouth. "But I will gladly…eagerly…accept other forms of payment."

"I'm not paying you with sex." That was her pride speaking, not her body. It was tingling in all the right places and more than willing to barter.

"I suppose, I could settle for a kiss." He moved closer, his breath tickling her lips.

She should stop him. She was not getting involved with another macho jerk, but it was just a kiss and she always paid her way. Her phone beeped and she jumped, looking down when it beeped again. Her friend was getting impatient.

"I guess you'd better get that." He was not happy.

As soon as Adrian got out of the car she could breathe again. It was like the man had stolen all the air, making her lightheaded, woozy even. She inhaled deeply, clearing her head. What in the hell had she been thinking? She couldn't kiss him no matter how much she wanted to. Her head was clear of passion, but her body still hummed. The man was only a few feet away at the pump and his ass looked yummy in those jeans. They were slightly faded and worn, conforming perfectly to his hips and butt. She wanted to unbutton those pants and feel him grow beneath her fingers. Then she'd unzip him, letting her knuckles graze his dick before pushing down those jeans and his underwear. She'd grab that nice ass with both hands, pulling him close to where she ached. He'd feel so good pressed hard and hot against her. Her phone beeped, breaking her out of her daydream. She sighed trembling slightly.

She needed to quit thinking like that or she was going to suggest they stop at one of those cheap hotels or even pull into a wooded area and get it on. Her phone beeped again, and she pulled it from her purse. Time to see what was so bloody important.

ALISON: Merry Christmas. How did it go last night?

ALISON: You can't still be sleeping. Call me. I NEED to know how last night went. I'm dying here.

ALISON: I'm at my mom's house. She's asking about my love life. I need to send her off the scent with yours. Give me bait, woman.

ALISON: Seriously. Text me back. I'm getting

worried.

ALISON: Text me now. Not kidding. Or I'll call your mom.

She sighed and texted.

ELLIE: I'm fine. Can't talk. Call you later.

ALISON: Thank God you're okay. I was getting ready to call 911.

Ellie shook her head. Her friend was the most annoying person she knew.

Adrian tapped on the window and then opened her door, putting his arm on the roof and leaning down by her. "I'm going inside. You wanna come?"

This was not helping. She'd been about ready to come just thinking about this man and now her olfactory senses were shoving her down memory lane. He smelled like fresh air and some outdoorsy, masculine scent. Last night, it'd surrounded her as she'd orgasmed—his hot body on top of hers, inside hers, giving her the most exquisite pleasure, his lips kissing her neck….and leaving a hickey. "No. I'll wait here."

"You know, you can come with me more than once." His green eyes sparkled mischievously.

"You did not just say—"

"If we stop again you can come with me…inside that

store too." A smile spread across his handsome face. "What did you think I meant?"

"You know…" Her phone beeped again. "Go. I'll wait here."

"You sure? You don't have to pee or anything?"

"No, I don't." Correction. Alison was the second most annoying person she knew.

CHAPTER 35: ADRIAN

"Do you want some coffee or something?" Adrian didn't want to leave Ellie smiling and texting that asshole Marc.

"I don't drink coffee."

"Really? Me either."

She looked up from her phone. "You don't? I thought I was the only person on the planet."

"Nope. Never liked the taste or the smell."

"Me either."

This should be a strange bonding moment, but she looked at him like he was playing a trick on her. "I can get you something else. Come inside with me and pick something out."

Her damn phone beeped again.

"No. Thanks. I'm fine." She looked back down, dismissing him.

He wanted to grab the phone and tell Marc to fuck off but instead he shut the door and walked into the gas station mumbling, "Women are so stupid. That guy humiliated her last night and now she's texting and smiling. I'm a fucking idiot."

After taking a piss he grabbed a water. He was horny, hungry, thirsty, irritated with the woman in his car and fucking tired as hell. He would've rather had spent the day in bed with Ellie, fucking and talking and sleeping. Why hadn't he met her on any other night besides Christmas Eve. He grabbed a bag of chips and then a Coke. He needed the caffeine.

He headed for the counter and stopped. He didn't care what she said, he couldn't go back to the car with nothing for her. It'd serve her right if he did, since she was smiling and texting her bonehead ex, but he couldn't do it. He put his items down on the counter. "I'm going to leave these here for a second."

"You want me to start ringing them up?" asked the old guy at the register.

The store was empty except for him. "Yeah. I need to get some other things."

He walked back to the coolers along the wall. He grabbed another water and then stared at the ton of different sodas and drinks. He had no idea what she liked. He couldn't even remember what she'd drank last night. He was pretty sure it'd had juice in it. He grabbed another Coke, a Sprite, a Dr. Pepper and an orange juice. He walked back to the counter and unloaded before turning and snatching another bag of chips and pretzels from the nearby rack.

"Long trip?" The clerk already had a bag ready and

was filling it with the items as he rang it up.

"Not really but I have no idea what she drinks or likes to eat."

The clerk looked around him out the window. "My wife likes the bags of mixed stuff."

"Mixed stuff?" He had no idea what that even was.

"That stuff." The clerk pointed to the bags of Chex Mix.

"Oh." He hadn't thought of those. There were a few different flavors. He had no idea which she'd prefer so he grabbed two different ones. "Can't hurt."

"Yeah, and if it makes her happy then"—the guy smiled wistfully—"you're happy."

"I suppose." He'd be happy if she'd agree to fuck him again instead of flirting with her asshole of an ex.

"Do whatever you can to make her happy, my boy. A happy woman makes a happy man." The older guy laughed. "Been married for thirty-five years. I know a thing or two."

"Thanks." He paid the guy, handing him an extra twenty. "Merry Christmas."

"Thank you. Merry Christmas."

He grabbed the bag and headed for the car. Ellie was no longer looking down at her phone. Hopefully, she'd told Marc to fuck off. He walked around to the driver's side, his gaze catching on the present from last night which had fallen on the floor behind his seat. He'd forgotten all about that. He got in the car, dropping the bag between them.

"Wow, you're hungry," she said.

"It's not all for me." He grabbed a water and a bag of chips before starting the car.

"You're taking this to your parents' house?" She was trying hard not to laugh. "Is this your contribution to Christmas dinner?"

"Hardly." He pulled out onto the highway. "I didn't know what you liked."

"You…" She glanced into the bag. "You bought all this for me?"

The clerk had been right. She may not be exactly happy—surprised, shocked, stunned were better adjectives—but under that was happiness and it made him feel like a hero. It also scared the shit out of him.

It was one thing to want her in a good mood, so she'd sleep with him again but when her moods started making his feelings change that wasn't good, not at all.

CHAPTER 36: ELLIE

Ellie stared into the bag filled with junk food. This was the sweetest thing anyone had ever done for her.

"I didn't buy it all for you." Adrian reached in the bag and snatched a Coke. "This is mine."

"Okay." Laughter bubbled out of her. She couldn't help it. Usually, he was suave and flirty. This prickly side of him was adorable. "There's another Coke in here. Is that yours too?"

"Nah." He stared straight ahead. "I didn't know what kind of soda you liked."

"Thank you." She grabbed the bottle. "I like Coke."

"Me too." He finished half of his water and opened the soda.

"Just like coffee."

"Yeah." He frowned.

"That's a bad thing?" She took a sip of her soda and pulled out the bag of Chex Mix.

"No. Just weird. Not the Coke thing. Lots of people like Coke but most people also like coffee."

"No kidding. I used to feel strange telling people that I didn't drink coffee but now, it doesn't bother me." She stared at the Chex Mix and then dropped it back into the bag.

"Wrong kind?"

"What?"

"The Chex Mix. I didn't know what you liked so I guessed and grabbed the original and cheese flavored ones. Did I get it wrong?"

"No. I like both of those, but my mom will kill me if I show up late and not hungry." Her stomach took that moment to grumble.

"I don't think a few chips are going to fill you up."

"Once I start eating those things I can't stop." She never bought them for that very reason. Her ass was wide enough as it was from sitting all day at work. She didn't need to feed her butt's urban sprawl.

"Open it. You can share with me." He tossed his bag of chips back in the big bag.

"Do you like Chex Mix?"

"Never had it."

He was so sweet. Her phone beeped and she glanced at it. Alison again. The woman was driving her crazy. "Eat the chips you like. I'm fine."

"Do you have to argue with me about everything? Just open the damn bag of Chex Mix."

"Don't yell at me." So much for him being sweet.

"Then for once do what I ask you to do."

"You didn't ask. You ordered." She had no idea why

he was being such a jerk. Actually, she did. This was typical for guys like him—charming when they wanted something and moody, super assholes when things didn't go their way.

"I didn't order you to open the Chex Mix."

"You didn't ask either." This time her phone rang. She was going to kill Alison. She pressed a button sending her friend to voicemail. She grabbed the Chex Mix and opened it. "There. Happy now?"

"Hardly." He gripped the steering wheel like it was the only thing keeping him from falling to his death or strangling her.

Her phone rang again.

"Don't let me stop you from answering it."

"I'm not." That wasn't completely true. Alison was going to drill her about last night and she didn't want to talk about Marc in front of Adrian. She sent Alison to voicemail again. Her friend wasn't going to be happy with her.

"Lying again."

"I'm not lying." Not exactly.

"Please. I saw you texting him earlier."

"Him?" What was he talking about?

"Marc."

"It's not Marc." Now, his grumpiness made sense.

"Right."

"It's not."

"Stop fucking lying. I'm not an idiot." He sent her a disgusted look. "You women are so fucking stupid. Putting up with shit like that from a guy."

"You women? Stupid?" She had no idea where to start being offended.

"Yeah. That bastard humiliated you last night."

"You should thank him."

"For what?" he almost shouted.

"Because…" She stopped herself. Saying she'd only slept with him because of her ex was true but it wasn't very nice.

"Because he's the reason you fucked me?" He snorted. "You can say it. It's not like I didn't know that."

Her phone rang again. "Damn it."

"Answer the fucking phone or I'll stop the car right here."

"You wouldn't." They were in the middle of nowhere.

He slammed on the brakes, pulling the car to the side of the road as her phone continued to ring. "Answer it. Tell him to fuck off or tell him you love him. Right now, I don't give two shits what you say, but you will answer that phone and you will stop hiding it from me."

She glared at him. He was the stupidest, bossiest man she'd ever met. "You want the phone answered? You do it." She shoved it in his face and waited. Both Adrian and Alison deserved this.

CHAPTER 37: ADRIAN

Adrian wanted nothing more than to yank the phone from Ellie's hand and tear Marc a new one, but he'd give her one warning. "Don't tempt me. I will do it."

"Go ahead."

He knew that tone. He'd heard every woman in his life use it at one time or another and it screamed *Warning*. *Warning* like the robot on Lost in Space.

When he was a kid, he'd witnessed his father ignore that tone and continue blithely on with the argument. It never ended well for his dad and he'd always wondered how his father could be so stupid but now he understood. Her tone didn't matter. The warning siren going off in his brain didn't matter. The only thing that did matter was finding an outlet for this raging frustration and disgust with her. How any woman could forgive a guy who'd treated her like Marc had was beyond him. He snatched the phone from her and pressed the button. "What the hell…"

"Ellie…You're not Ellie," said a woman. "Marc? Is that you?"

"Fuck no, I'm not Marc and neither are you." He couldn't help it he grinned. For once Ellie hadn't lied to him. "Uhm…I'm sorry about yelling. I thought—"

"Who are you?"

"I'm Adrian. Who are you?" Suddenly, life was good. Ellie hadn't been texting with her ex.

"Where's Ellie?"

"Right here." He handed the phone to her.

She sat with her arms crossed over her chest. She wasn't nearly as happy about this as he was.

"Ellie, it's for you." He thought she'd smile or at least acknowledge him, but she glared straight ahead. "Uhm…it's not Marc." He gave her his best silly grin, hoping for a hint of a smile or some sparkle of amusement in her eyes.

She turned toward him, her eyes hard and unblinking like a snake waiting to strike. "I told you that."

"Ellie? Ellie, are you okay? Who is this guy?" yelled the woman on the phone.

"And I told *you* that I'd call you back later." She directed this at the phone.

He took some satisfaction in the fact that Ellie was as mad at this woman as she was with him. "Take it." He waved the phone at her. "She wants to talk to you."

"I know and I told her I'd call her later. Just like I told you it wasn't Marc."

"What did she say?" asked the woman. "I can barely hear her."

"Take this so I can drive." He waved the phone at her

again.

"No."

"What was that? I can't hear you," said the woman.

"Hold on." He pressed a button and put the phone on speaker before hooking it into the phone cradle on the car. "It seems that Ellie isn't going to take the phone, so I put you on speaker, Miss?"

"Alison," said the woman. "Ellie, are you okay?"

"I'm fine," she said through gritted teeth. "Like I said when I texted you at least five times."

"I know but I'm going crazy at my mom's house and I wanted to talk to you."

"I was going to call as soon as I got to my parents' house."

"You're not there yet? What happened last night? And who is this guy you're with?"

"No, I'm not there. Marc and I broke up last night and—"

"You broke up? What happened? Are you okay?" Alison paused for half a heartbeat. "You already found another guy? Good for you. How did you do that? I'd never be that lucky. Is he good looking? Wait. You're still with him. Did you and he…Oh, my God."

"Stop." Ellie reached for the phone, but he snatched it from the cradle.

"Oh, no. I definitely want to hear the answers to some of those questions."

"Give me my phone." Ellie almost snarled.

"Nope." He slowed the car down again.

"What are you doing?" Ellie was not happy.

"What's he doing? Is he trying to kiss you? Are you going to let him? Let him. Definitely let him," rambled Alison.

He laughed. "No, I'm not trying to kiss her. I'm driving and if she doesn't behave and agree to leave the phone in the cradle then I'll have to stop the car. I don't want to get in an accident."

"Give me my phone," repeated Ellie.

"I offered but you didn't want it." He grinned at her. "Actually, she didn't want to talk to either of us. So, how about we talk?"

"Alison, hang up the phone. Right now," said Ellie.

"If you do that Alison, you know she'll never answer your questions. Not all of them."

"You're right. He's right," said Alison.

"Ellie, if you promise to behave and leave the phone in the cradle, I'll leave it on speaker so you can hear." He glanced at her. "Will you behave?"

"It's my phone."

"I'll take that as a no."

"I really want to talk to both of you, " said Alison. "Please Ellie, behave."

"Behave? I am behaving. He's the one who stole my phone."

"You gave it to me," he corrected.

"Because you were being a jerk."

"I thought it was Marc."

"And you were jealous," said Alison. "That is so

sweet."

"I wasn't jealous. I just don't like women being stupid."

"Excuse me?" Now, Alison wasn't happy with him either.

Maybe his sisters were right, and he did have a knack for pissing off the opposite sex. It didn't matter because this time he was right. "Marc treated her like shit last night."

"What did he do?" asked Alison.

He glanced at Ellie. Her face was pale and her lips tight. If she were sad instead of angry, she'd looked exactly like she had when he'd first noticed her at the Club. "She can tell you that later but take my word, he was a jerk."

"How did you two meet?"

"At the"—another glance at Ellie but her face had relaxed—"Club."

"The sex club?" Alison whispered like she was a child saying a bad word.

"Yes." He laughed. "At La Petite Mort Club."

"What's it like?"

"It's a club," said Ellie. "Filled with rich, arrogant jerks like Adrian."

"Hey. I saved you."

"Oh, do tell," said Alison.

"I need to either pull over or put the phone in the cradle." He glanced at Ellie. "Which is it?"

"Fine. I won't touch my phone."

"What do you think, Alison. Should I trust her?"

"Hmm. I don't know," said Alison. "She tends to lie about things like this."

"Hey," said Ellie.

He burst out laughing. "So, she doesn't just lie to me. I guess I pull over."

"You could tie her hands together," suggested Alison.

Adrian almost dropped the phone as his dick shot up like a Jack-in-the-box.

"What?" Ellie shouted. "I can't believe you said that."

"I like your friend." His voice had grown gruff with desire. "I really, really like your friend."

CHAPTER 38: ELLIE

"That makes one of us." Ellie usually found Alison's quick wit and inability to keep one thought to herself extremely amusing but not when it was directed at her.

"Oh, you know you love me," said Alison. "And don't pretend you wouldn't like being tied up. You told me—"

"Shut up," Ellie almost growled and somehow her less than sensitive friend heard the warning.

"Oh, right. I guess I shouldn't say that around strangers."

"We aren't exactly strangers." Adrian's voice was like warm brandy, heating her blood and making her brain foggy.

"Oh, so you two did shake the sheets." Alison sounded impressed. "I can't believe you picked up a stranger, Ellie. I've always wanted to do that. Alone at a bar. Pick up a handsome stranger and…What does he look like? I need to see him."

"Oh god, kill me now," muttered Ellie.

"Was he good in bed? How many times did you do it?"

"Aren't you going to answer your friend?" asked Adrian.

"I don't have a friend. Not anymore."

"Oh, you don't mean that." Alison laughed. "She doesn't. She just gets annoyed with me."

"Me too." He chuckled as he pulled over and stopped the car. '

"What are you doing?" asked Ellie. "I haven't even tried to touch the phone and we all know I've had plenty of reasons."

"Your friend wants to see me." He spoke into the phone. "You want a picture or a video chat?"

"It's not safe to drive and video chat," said Ellie. "And I'm not sitting on the side of the road while you two yap to each other." This trip was turning into a nightmare she couldn't escape.

"Picture it is." He held out the phone, leaning toward her. "Want to take a selfie with me?"

"No." She shoved him back to his side of the car. She should get out and walk home. It'd take forever and it was cold, but it'd be better than staying here. She knew exactly what was coming as soon as Alison saw him.

"Okay." He smiled and snapped a selfie and then texted it to Alison before putting the phone back in the cradle and pulling onto the road.

"Oh my god, he's gorgeous. You had sex with this man? You are so lucky," said Alison.

"I'm going to say this again. I really, really like your friend."

The smugness in his tone made Ellie want to puke.

"And I like you," said Alison.

"Then why don't you two hookup and leave me alone?" She may have said it but the thought of that happening made her stomach twist.

"I'd be tempted if you hadn't already tapped this stud," joked Alison.

"Can a woman tap a man?" He frowned. "Tapping implies breaking a seal and a man—"

"Okay, rode that steed. Is that better?" asked Alison.

"Makes more sense but I prefer stud or stallion."

"Would the two of you please stop." Ellie touched her temple. She was going to have a migraine if they kept it up.

"Since you won't answer my questions," said Alison. "I have to get the information somehow."

"No, you don't but you win. You want your questions answered? I'll do my best, but you've thrown out eight thousand of them." Ellie had had enough. "Let me see if I can get the highlights. Yes, Marc and I broke up. Yes, he's an asshole and was a complete shit last night. Yes, I picked up a strange guy in the sex club and slept with him."

"Ah-hem." Adrian cleared his throat and said in a low, side voice, "Several times. We had sex several times."

"Really?" asked Alison. "How many times exactly?"

"Two." Ellie was pretty sure her teeth were going to grind into dust. "We had sex two times."

"I think for you it was three," he muttered.

"Don't." She gave him a glare even his stubborn ass had to understand. "And yes, he's good looking."

The arrogant ass actually sat up straighter and if he hadn't been driving, she would've clawed that stupid grin off his face.

"Uhm…how was he?" Alison whispered.

"He can hear you," said Ellie. "You're on speakerphone. Remember?"

"That's why I whispered."

"It wasn't quiet enough. It'll never be quiet enough on speakerphone." Ellie wanted to slam her head against the dashboard.

"I don't mind if you answer." He shot her an even cockier grin.

She was so done with both of them. "It was fine."

"Ouch," said Alison. "That was harsh. You know, he can hear you."

"She's lying. Trust me. It was better than fine."

"Maybe for you, but it doesn't seem like it was that good for her," said Alison. "Did you take your time? Unlike men, women need to get their engines humming. They need a slow—"

"I know what women need." His cocky grin slid from his face. "And yes, I took my time."

"Not the first time. We didn't even get our clothes off." She was starting to enjoy this conversation.

"Oh," said Alison. "I'm not sure if that's hot or awful. Which was it?"

"Hot." He sent Ellie a look that dared her to deny it.

It had been hot, but she'd had enough of his arrogance and she never backed down from a challenge. "It was fine."

"Double ouch." Alison even sounded like she was wincing. "It's okay, Adrian. You can learn what you need to do. It just takes practice."

"I know what to do." His fingers gripped the wheel so tight Ellie was pretty sure his arms were shaking.

"Still like my friend?" She couldn't keep from smiling if she tried and she wasn't trying. "Do you still really, really like her?"

CHAPTER 39: ADRIAN

"This is not her fault." Adrian was no longer fond of this Alison woman anymore—AT ALL—but he refused to admit that to Ellie. This was war now and he wasn't going to let her win even one tiny battle. "It's yours."

"Uhm, Adrian," said Alison. "I think it's actually your fault. Yes, the woman is somewhat responsible for her own orgasm but if the guy is too fast…well…"

"I was not too fast." Okay, that first time had been a little quick but…"She came."

"Is that true, Ellie?" asked Alison.

"Do not lie about this." He'd stop the car and paddle her ass if she did.

"Sure. Of course, I did." Her tone said the opposite.

"Oh…I'm so sorry, Ellie," said Alison.

"You dirty, little liar." He almost laughed. He'd had no idea she was this conniving. "You came so hard you screamed."

"He confused a yawn with a scream." Ellie gave him a superior look.

"I did not. You screamed. Loud."

"I'm sure she did." Alison's voice was placating. "But women can fake it, you know."

"She did not fake it." No way. He would've known.

"Are you sure?" asked Alison.

"Yes." He knew this. This was fact. "I felt it...intimately." Her pussy had squeezed his cock like she was never letting it go and it'd felt fucking fantastic. He was getting hard just thinking about it.

"Oh, we can fake that too." Alison's chipper voice and Ellie's amused expression made him want to break something. "Once I laid there moaning and practicing my Kegels but, in my head, I wanted the guy to hurry up and finish. I'm sure he thought he was doing me a favor by not coming too soon but it was the worst few minutes of my life."

"She did not fake it." His hands tightened on the steering wheel.

"Okay. Let's move on. That's in the past."

"It certainly is," mumbled Ellie.

"That wasn't nice," said Alison. "We're trying to help Adrian not embarrass him."

He glanced at Ellie because he had no one else and mouthed, "Is she for real?"

Ellie nodded, her lush lips turning upward in a small, sexy smile.

"It's weird," Alison continued. "I always thought that guys who looked like him would be great in bed."

"I am great in bed."

"I'm sure you are." It was clear from Alison's tone that she was sure of the exact opposite. "But one can always improve with practice."

"Now, that's an excellent idea." He took a drink of his soda. "We should stop at one of these hotels and have a quick go. Apparently, I'm fast and could use the practice."

"That's not a bad idea," said Alison.

"That's a horrible idea and it's not going to happen." Ellie gave him a disbelieving look.

"Why? You had sex with him last night. One more time won't hurt, and you can help him improve. Give him some pointers."

"Yeah, Ellie. Give me some pointers. If I remember correctly you like being in charge."

"How would you know? That never happened."

"Hmm. You're right. Let's pull over and correct that." He was more than ready but there was no way she was running the show. She'd probably screw it all up, not orgasm and then it'd be his fault again. Damn it. Not again. She had come. He was not wrong about that. He wasn't.

"No. Absolutely not." Ellie growled. "Keep driving. I'm already late and now I have a headache."

"Sex can help get rid of a headache," he said.

"He's right," said Alison. "I read that."

"Not this headache," said Ellie. "The only way to help this headache is getting away from the two of you."

"Now, you've hurt my feelings." Alison laughed. "Or you would but I know you love me." She clapped. "I got it. Adrian, you should watch porn. That'd help. I know it helped me learn how to give a better blow job. Ellie too."

"Alison. Shut up," hissed Ellie.

His head snapped toward her. "You watch porn…for instructions?" He'd been wrong. His dick hadn't been hard before, not compared to this. If he thought about her touching herself while she watched porn, he'd come in his pants.

"Oh…Aunt Tiff is here." Alison sounded like she'd moved her face away from the phone. "I've gotta run."

"Thank god," muttered Ellie.

"Oh…oh…wait," said Alison

"Now what?" Ellie leaned her head against the back of her seat. "I truly don't think I can take much more."

"I have tickets for The Blue Newb."

"The new night club?" Ellie sat up. "How did you get tickets?"

"Gus."

"Gus? As in your boss Mr. Harker? When did he become Gus?"

"When he made me work Christmas Eve. You should see his face when I call him Gus. He absolutely hates it." Alison laughed.

"But he gave you tickets to the hottest night club in town?"

"Yeah, for New Year's Eve." Alison squealed. "Tell me you'll go with me. Please, please."

"Absolutely. That sounds great."

"Adrian, do you want to go too?" asked Alison. "I already asked Gus to get another ticket for—"

"No," Ellie snapped.

"That was rude," said Alison.

Adrian choked on his drink. Alison had no room to talk but he quickly cleared his throat because this time she was on his side.

"The poor guy is driving you all the way to your parents' house on Christmas and…well…you haven't been very nice to him."

"She's been mean to me since I met her." He used the saddest, poutiest tone he knew.

"Oh, that's awful," said Alison.

"I have not been mean to you since I met you."

"I guess, that's your opinion, but you've heard her, Alison. What do you think?" He fought to keep the sad expression on his face. "All I've wanted to do from the moment I saw her was to make her smile and…"

"Aww, that's so sweet," cooed Alison.

"That's not at all you wanted," Ellie whispered in a harsh tone.

"But it was." This time he didn't have to pretend, and it must've shown because he felt Ellie's gaze on him, searching for the truth.

"Fine. See if you can get him a ticket but this doesn't mean that we're going together or having sex or anything."

"Are you sure about that?" he teased.

"Positive. Absolutely positive."

"Great. I'll remind Harker that I need one more ticket," said Alison.

"Uhm…thanks but don't go to the trouble. I can't go.

I'm staying at my parents' until after New Year's Day." He braced himself for Ellie's outcry, trying not to smile but she was so much fun to annoy.

CHAPTER 40: ELLIE

"You can't go? Then why did you…." Ellie counted to ten in her head. Adrian was driving her absolutely bonkers. Her body, however, was a tad disappointed it wouldn't be seeing him again on New Year's Eve but it was for the best. She was pretty sure that as soon as alcohol clouded her brain she'd be back in that man's bed and she couldn't let that happen.

"That's too bad," said Alison. "I really wanted to meet you but maybe some other time."

"I'm sure we'll be seeing each other." He gave Ellie a look that said he wasn't just talking to Alison.

"I'm sure we won't."

"Ellie, you should be nicer to the man. He's helping you out…a lot."

"Your friend is a wise woman," he said.

There were voices in the background on the phone.

"I've gotta go. Merry Christmas." Alison hung up.

Ellie almost sank into the seat.

"Your friend is…a bit of a whirlwind."

Since there was humor and a hint of fondness in his tone, Ellie decided not to take offense. Alison was a terror sometimes, but she was Ellie's best friend. "She is. I love her but she has no filter."

"She certainly doesn't." He laughed. "She's a lot of fun."

"Yeah, it's a blast when she's directing all that…whatever you call it…at someone else. Not as much fun when it's coming your way."

"No. That's not fun at all, but it's still funny." He turned on the radio. "Let me find some more Christmas music to put you in the mood."

She couldn't help it; she laughed. "You have a one-track mind."

"That was before. Now, it's a mission. I have to prove to both of us that you didn't fake it."

"That is so not going to happen." But a small part of her—pretty much the part between her legs—wanted it to. Again and again.

"Oh, it is so going to happen." His tone wasn't at all teasing and the roughness made her blood heat. "Do you really watch porn for instructional purposes?"

"No." She did but she wasn't going to admit that to him.

"Liar." He glanced at her. "You should do something about that. You lie a lot."

"I do not."

"Speaking of porn." He slowed the car, stopping at a stop sign.

"Let's not." The thought of porn and Adrian was a potent combination.

"You still have a gift to open." He leaned into the back seat.

"A gift?"

He dropped the present from the Mistletoe Game onto her lap and started driving again.

"Oh...that."

"Yeah. Shame we forgot about it last night but we'll use whatever it is the next time."

"There won't be a next time."

"Keep telling yourself that." One side of his mouth turned up in that annoying smirk.

"You are unbelievable."

"Unbelievably good in bed, no matter how much you lie about it." He nudged her arm with his elbow. "Open it unless you want to wait until we're at your parents' house?"

"Good lord, no." She started unwrapping it, taking her time not to ruin the paper. It was even prettier in the light—dark green and gold. She removed the paper, folded it and placed it between them before staring at the box. "Desiree gave us a vibrator?"

He glanced at it. "That would've been fun. Correction. That will be fun."

"Why would...these are for..." She stopped at his amused expression.

"You've never played with a vibrator wi—"

"Of course, I have." The words were out before she

could stop them.

"Now, that's a real shame."

"Why? You can't tell me you don't masturbate." She refused to be embarrassed but she couldn't stop her face from heating.

"Of course, I masturbate. We all do. It's natural." His eyes roamed over her. "And it's super-hot when a woman isn't ashamed of doing it but what is a shame is you masturbating alone."

"Alone? There isn't any other way. I mean, that's the definition of the word."

"You've never played with one of these with a partner." It wasn't a question.

"Why would a man want that in bed with him?" She was starting to feel a little out of her league.

"To please you." His voice was rougher, deeper, bringing back flashes of last night—that voice in her ear whispering, teasing as he thrust inside her.

"I thought that's what the man was for." She tried to be flippant, but it fell flat.

"It is but men are limited. Once they come, they're done for bit. Women on the other hand…are lucky. With the right partner they can come over and over, like I proved to you last night. If we'd had this, I would've made you come at least two more times." He glanced at her. "You don't believe me and I can't wait to show you what you've been missing." He grabbed the box, his fingers skimming softly along her thigh. "And this is more than just a vibrator."

"What else is it?" Her throat was dry, and her body started to tighten with desire. She really wanted him to move those talented fingers between her thighs.

"It can be used remotely using Wi-Fi and a phone." He stopped the car on the side of the road a few yards from her parents' house.

"What are you doing? Why are you stopping." As much as she wanted his hand between her legs, it couldn't happen. It was daylight and she was in the neighborhood where she'd grown up.

"One second." He had his phone in his hand. "Let me download the app." He picked up the present, looking at the box and then typed something into his phone before handing the box to her. "I want you to put this in."

"In? In where?"

"You know." His wicked grin made her almost overheat.

"I am not going to do that." But wetness pooled between her legs.

"Yes, you are. You're going to put it in and leave it inside you. You'll never know when I'll turn this on." He pressed a button on his phone and the toy vibrated. "It could start at any time, any strength, and any duration. Soft pulses over and over." He touched his phone and the toy hummed quietly. "One quick burst, lighting you on fire and then another." The toy shook in the box. "Anything I can think of…hard, long, quick, slow." He took the toy through its paces as he spoke.

Ellie couldn't tear her eyes away from it, imagining

how it'd feel.

"You'll be on edge all day, wondering when the next burst of pleasure will fill you. You'll think of me every second because it may not be my dick inside you, but it will be me fucking you." His tone was rich and mesmerizing.

"I can't," she whispered.

"You can." He rested the toy on her thigh near the juncture of her legs. "You want to."

"No." She shoved all the passion that was making her brain fuzzy aside. "I'm not going to be…aroused…while celebrating Christmas with my family."

"Oh…yeah. Right." He frowned but then his eyes brightened. "Put it in tonight when you go to bed then call me."

"No." She lifted the vibrator off her leg and dropped it in the box. "I'm not using that ever." She tossed the present into the back seat. She was going to find a nice, sweet guy who was interested in her not just in having sex with her.

"Never say never." He pulled back onto the road. "Challenge accepted."

"That was not a chall…" She clamped her mouth shut, arguing with him was pointless. They were only a few minutes from her parents' house. She'd thank him for the ride and walk away. Challenge won.

CHAPTER 41: ADRIAN

If Adrian were a different kind of guy he'd be insulted. Ellie was leaning forward in her seat, purse and overnight bag, which she'd grabbed from the back seat, on her lap.

"Why are you driving so slow?" she asked.

"I thought you were going to jump out of the car."

"What?" Her head snapped toward him. "Why would I do that?"

"I don't know. You've got all your stuff. Your hand is on the door." He shrugged. "I slowed down so you wouldn't get hurt." He winked at her because he knew it would make her crazy. "I'm a nice guy like that. Always thinking of you."

"Yeah, you're a prince."

"Thank you." He sat up straighter. "I think so."

"You..." She took a deep calming breath and then said, "I'm not jumping out of a moving vehicle so you can put your foot down on the gas pedal. I swear that old man with the walker is going to pass us."

"I'm not going that slow." He had slowed down but it

was because they were in a subdivision, not because he was dreading the end of this odd but amusing journey.

The guy with the walker moved closer. He was almost to the back bumper.

Okay, maybe he should step on it a bit. He pushed his foot down a little for another few yards before turning into the driveway of a very nice house. He hadn't thought about it, but he wasn't surprised that Ellie came from an upper middle-class family. She was the type—hard working but not afraid to spend money on clothes, purses, etc.

He on the other hand was just learning to do that. He'd grown up middle class, sometimes lower middle class, depending on what life had thrown their way. Yet they'd always had everything they'd needed, and he and his sisters had learned at a young age to work for what they wanted. He put the car in park.

"Don't turn it off." She said quickly as she jumped out the door.

"You sure you don't want me to come in and say howdy to Mom and Pops." He couldn't wait to see her bristle like a baby badger—ferocious but so fucking cute.

"No. I mean, yes, I'm sure." She glanced at the door to the house before leaning back into the car. "Thank you. I mean it. For everything."

Her cheeks flushed a little, but he wasn't sure if it was from the cold or the memories of last night. He knew those memories sure made him hot…and hard.

"You're welcome. Anytime." He grinned. "I mean that. Anytime you want to take out some frustration and go for a ride…I'm available."

"I appreciate that, but it won't happen again."

"I think you're wrong." He'd do everything he could to make sure she was wrong about that. "I don't think fate is done with us yet."

"Please." She scoffed. "This had nothing to do with fate and everything to do with my asshole ex."

"I can't argue with that." He was too glad she was still referring to the jerk as an ex to argue. "Seriously though, I could give you a call when I come back into town. We could go to dinner or—"

"No. I can't. Goodbye, Adrian and thanks." She turned and started to shut the door.

"Wait."

She hesitated.

"Don't forget your present." He held out the toy from La Petite Mort Club.

"I'm not taking that." She looked at him like he was handing her a dead puppy.

"You sure?" He did his best to not smile. "You might need it for your frustrations. You know, since we're done and all."

"Yes, I'm positive," she almost hissed before slamming the door and striding toward the house.

He was going to wait to make sure she got inside because he was a gentleman and because he enjoyed watching those hips sway and that ass jiggle. She spun around when she was a few feet from the house, waving him away. He pretended not to understand and waved back, loving how her face pinched up with annoyance. She flipped her hand in a "get out of here" gesture and mouthed, go away.

He laughed and glanced down to put the car in reverse. "Shit. She forgot her phone." He rolled down the window. "Ellie. Wait."

"No." She kept walking toward the door.

"Seriously. Stop." He got out of the car, her phone in his hand.

CHAPTER 42: ELLIE

Ellie was not turning around. She was done with Adrian and his jokes. She raised her hand over her shoulder and waved. "Thanks again. Bye." She walked faster, hurrying up the stairs and praying he'd take the hint and leave. She reached for the door, but it opened before she could grab the handle.

"Ellie. You finally made it." Her brother Robbie stood in the doorway a bag of trash in his hand.

"Merry Christmas to you too." She gave him a half-hug, avoiding the garbage. He'd filled out so much since the last time she'd seen him. He looked like a man now, no longer a gangly boy. "You look great."

"Thanks. Been working out and..." He glanced over her shoulder, his face bunching up. "Who's that?"

"No one. A friend." She started to push past him.

"I think he wants to talk to you."

"Too bad. We've talked enough for the day."

"He's heading this way."

"He wouldn't." She spun around. He would. He was.

She was going to kill him.

"Robbie why are you standing in the doorway. Take out the trash," yelled her mother from inside the house.

She turned toward her brother, pulling him onto the porch and shutting the door behind him. "Do not say anything to her about this." She started down the stairs to stop Adrian before he could get any closer. She needed to get him out of there before her mother saw him.

"Mom," yelled Robbie, holding the door partially open. "Ellie's here and she brought her new boyfriend."

Adrian stopped in the middle of the sidewalk, his eyes widening with surprise.

Robbie walked past her, giving her a superior look before turning to Adrian. "Sorry, dude. Couldn't let the opportunity pass."

"I have six sisters. I completely understand." He slid something into his back pocket and the two shook hands, grinning like long lost pals.

"Sisters aren't the problem. Try having a brother," muttered Ellie.

"Brothers are a girl's blessing," said Adrian.

Robbie barked a laugh, but it died at the serious expression on Adrian's face.

"Pl...eese. All men are a girl's worst nightmare, especially brothers," she said.

"Hey," said Robbie. "I'm standing right here."

"And you betrayed me."

"Ellie?" Mom said from the doorway.

Ellie flinched. There was no escaping now. She turned

around and hurried back toward the house. "Mom. Merry Christmas."

Her mother met her halfway, pulling her into a warm hug. Ellie sighed, clinging to her mother. Mom gave the best hugs. They were warm and strong and filled with love.

"Ellie." Mom kissed her cheek. "I'm sorry to hear about you and Marc but we can talk about that later." She let go and smiled, warm and welcoming. "First, introduce me to your new friend."

CHAPTER 43: ADRIAN

Adrian hadn't meant for this to happen, but he was loving every minute. He'd never minded meeting "the parents." Parents loved him. He was attractive, polite, funny and he treated their daughters like princesses—in public. They definitely didn't want to know how he treated them in private. Their hair would turn even grayer but this mom wasn't gray. She was hot. If Ellie aged like her mother whomever married her would be one lucky SOB.

"Mom, this is Adrian. He gave me a ride home. Adrian, this is my mom, Elizabeth." Ellie raced through the introductions. "But he can't stay. He has to go. Now. Because—"

"Nice to meet you, ma'am." He held out his hand, ignoring Ellie.

"It's nice to meet you too. Please, call me Liz." Ellie's mom took his hand in both of hers. "Thank you so much for bringing my daughter home on Christmas."

"My pleasure."

Ellie snorted.

He kept his face impassive, but it was hard especially at the confused look Liz gave her daughter.

"Is that Ellie?" A man stepped out of the house.

"Dad." She ran to her father, hugging him. It didn't surprise Adrian that she was a daddy's girl.

"Please, come inside," said Liz. "It's too cold to stay out here."

"Yes, come inside," said the dad, his arm still around Ellie.

"He can't," said Ellie. "He has to get to his parents' house."

"Surely, you can come in for a minute or two," said Liz. "I'll get you some coffee for your trip. I hope you don't have far to go."

"He doesn't like coffee," blurted Ellie.

"I can't believe there are two of you on the planet who don't drink coffee," joked her father.

"I can get you something else hot. Tea. Hot chocolate?" asked Liz.

"Mom, he needs to get home to his family," said Ellie.

"It'll only take a minute." Liz took his arm.

He followed her into the house, sending Ellie a helpless look. She gave him a death glare and he shrugged. What was he supposed to do?

"Who's that?" asked a petite, blonde woman as she came down the stairs.

"Tina, this is Adrian, my friend." Ellie stressed the last word. "Marc still has my car, so Adrian gave me a ride home on his way to his parents' house, but he can't stay."

"Hi," said Tina. "Where do your parents live?"

"In Cedar Ridge," he said.

"Oh my, that's like an hour drive," said Liz. "You have to take a sandwich or something." She dropped her hand from his arm and headed for the kitchen.

Ellie sent him another glare.

He decided to take pity on her. "Thanks, but my mom will kill me if I'm not hungry when I get there."

"I'll make a small one for you," said Liz.

"I'm Craig." The father held out his hand. "Thank you for going out of your way to bring Ellie home on Christmas. It's been a while since we've all been together."

"It was no problem, sir." He shook Craig's hand. "It was nice having company for the trip."

"We should probably head into the kitchen before Liz prepares a meal for you," said Craig.

"I heard that," yelled Liz.

"Am I wrong?" Craig laughed as he walked into the kitchen.

He looked at Ellie for guidance and she rolled her eyes and headed for the kitchen. He and Tina followed. Robbie plopped down on the couch and started playing video games.

"Was the traffic bad?" Craig's hand trailed over Liz's lower back as he walked to the cabinet and pulled out a travel mug.

"No, and thanks but I'll just have water." He studied them. There was something familiar about the couple. It was in the way they moved together and interacted with each other.

"Nothing warm?" Liz continued to make the sandwich.

"No thank you, ma'am. Water would be nice though."

Craig put the travel mug back and grabbed a bottle of water from the refrigerator. He handed it to Adrian before starting to help Liz at the counter, his hand softly brushing against her arm.

Damn it. He knew them but he had no idea from where. "Have we met?"

Craig paused, looking more closely at him. "You do look familiar."

Liz finished the sandwich and studied him. "He does."

"What do you do for a living?" asked Craig. "I own an advertising business. Maybe we've met there."

"Don't think so. I work in cyber security, definitely not an ads guy."

"Hmm." Craig leaned against the counter, his hand on Liz's arm, his thumb softly skimming over her skin.

She put the sandwich on a plate before staring up at her husband, her gaze filled with so much love and contentment that it was almost sensual.

That was it. He had seen them before…at the Club. His eyes darted to Ellie. There was no way she knew, and he wasn't going to be the one to tell her that her parents frequented and often played on stage at La Petite Mort Club. Not only could he lose his membership by exposing another member, but he also couldn't do that to Ellie.

"Is something the matter?" asked Liz.

"No." He smiled. "But if that's a small sandwich I'd

hate to see your large one."

She laughed. "Nonsense." She took the plate to the table. "Sit. Eat."

Ellie's face was pinched. He'd enjoyed teasing her about meeting her parents, but he'd never intended to go through with it.

"I can't. My mom and dad are waiting."

"Oh, right. I'm sorry." Liz handed him the plate.

He started to take the sandwich.

"No, take the plate. You can give it to Ellie next time you see her. That'll give her a reason to come and see us."

"Mom, it hasn't been that long."

"Two Christmas's ago," said Liz.

He hated this argument. He'd had it with his mother too many times to count. "Thanks, but I'm not sure when I'll see Ellie again."

She turned to him, surprise warring with gratitude in her eyes.

"We just sort of bumped into each other last night and—"

Tina snickered and for once Ellie's glare wasn't directed at him.

"What?" Tina glanced at them. "It's a funny meme. You want to see it?" She waved her phone at them, but she hadn't been looking at her phone when she'd laughed. The only ones who probably didn't realize that were Craig and Liz since Tina was standing behind them.

"Speaking of phones," he pulled Ellie's from his pocket. "This is what I was trying to give to you earlier."

"Oh." Her face softened. "I thought…"

"I know." He handed her the plate and the phone. "I do have to get going."

"I'll walk you out," she said.

He nodded. It wasn't much but it was a start. He looked at Liz. "Thank you for the water and the sandwich."

"You're welcome. Have a safe trip and tell your parents that they raised a wonderful young man," said Liz.

"They'll be pleased to hear it." He smiled and followed Ellie out of house. Neither of them said anything until they stopped at his car. He opened the passenger side and put the water and sandwich on the seat before closing the door and turning to Ellie. "I didn't mean for this to happen. I just wanted to give you your phone."

"I know that now." She glanced up at him, a sparkle in her brown eyes. "I just hope the voodoo curse I placed on you doesn't work."

He laughed. "What was it? I need to know so I can circumvent the danger."

"The usual." She waved her hand in a dismissive way. "You know, a slow and painful death. Stuff like that."

"For meeting your parents? You have a violent side. You should see someone about that." He tried hard to keep from laughing but he was a good-natured guy and he liked playful Ellie.

"Seriously, though. Thank you for everything," she said.

"But especially for not staying for Christmas dinner, right?" He joked because he wasn't quite ready to say goodbye.

"Yes, especially that." She laughed and he drank in the sight.

The sunlight shimmered in her hair, making it almost gold, and her lips were full and lush, begging for him to taste them.

"And"—she sobered—"for everything else. The ride out here. The snacks…and last night." Her hand touched his chest, and he was sure she could feel the thudding of his heart as she stood on her tiptoes and kissed his cheek. "Merry Christmas, Adrian."

"Merry Christmas, Ellie." His hands rested on her hips. He wanted to pull her close and kiss her until time and space vanished, but she didn't want that…not right now. He could feel it in the tension of her body, so he kissed her forehead.

She relaxed into him for a second before she stepped away. "I should get back inside. I'm sure they're all watching us out the window."

"Yeah." He didn't care if the whole world watched them.

"Bye." She turned and started toward the house.

He opened the car door. "Wait," he hollered, smiling as he saw her back stiffen but this time she turned around. He grabbed the wrapping paper that she'd folded so neatly and walked over to her. He took her hand. "I want you to have this."

"I'm not taking…"

He put the paper in her palm. "A memory of our night

together."

CHAPTER 44: ELLIE

Ellie walked inside the house, clutching that small bit of wrapping paper in her hand like it'd disappear if she loosened her grip for one second.

"You have got to tell me what happened." Tina grabbed her arm and pulled her toward the stairs.

Her mom and dad were in the kitchen and her brother still sat on the couch, completely lost in the video game.

"I'm surprised everyone wasn't watching out the window."

"They were." Tina ducked into the room that used to be theirs. "Except for Robbie. He doesn't care about anything but video games." Her tone was disgusted. "He seems so grown up except for that."

"Marc still plays them. I don't think males ever grow up from that."

"Trevor doesn't play them anymore. He's been under a lot of stress at work." Tina frowned.

"Where is he?" She used to like Trevor but the longer he strung her sister along, never agreeing to set a date for the wedding, the more her patience with the man waned.

"He should be here soon. He had to work last night."

"Oh. Good. I'm glad he's going to be able to make it this year." It'd make Tina happy, so she was happy.

"Now, tell me about Adrian."

"Nothing much to tell." She shrugged.

"Nothing much is not a word you ever use about a man like that." Tina grabbed her arm, yanking her to the bed. "Spill. I mean it."

"Seriously, there's not much to say." At least not much she wanted to discuss, but her sister was like a terrier. She had to give her something and it was best to stay as close to the truth as possible. "I met him last night. He just happened to be there when Marc and I broke up."

"What happened?"

"He was cheating on me." Her voice cracked. Why did they always cheat on her? Every last one of them.

"Oh, Ellie." Tina hugged her. "I'm so sorry. That jerk doesn't deserve you."

"I know...but..."

"Don't you dare say it." Tina leaned back and it was like looking into her father's green eyes. "You did nothing wrong. His cheating is because of him, not you."

They'd been over this when her college boyfriend had cheated. "But all of them? Every guy I've ever dated has cheated on me. Logic would say that it does have something to do with me."

"You and your logic." Tina may have her father's eyes, but she was a romantic like their mother. "The only thing you're doing wrong is picking the wrong guy."

"I agree with that. I'm done with these macho jerks." Too bad she hadn't met Adrian before Marc. They would've had fun for a bit…until he eventually cheated on her.

"Agreed. So, tell me more about Adrian. He seems nice and he is gorgeous." Tina fanned her face.

"Again. Nothing to tell. We met last night when I was waiting for Marc and then he gave me a ride home." *Several glorious rides to be exact.* "That's it."

"That's it?"

"Yeah." She was having a hard time figuring out if her sister was disappointed or setting a trap. Tina was a pretty darn good actor.

"Did you spend the night with him?"

"No." That wasn't technically a lie. By the time they'd arrived at his place it'd almost been today.

"He stayed with you?"

"No." That was completely true.

"Then how was he there to give you a ride out here?"

"Ah…" This was almost as bad as being interrogated by her father when she'd been a kid.

"You'd better think faster than that if you don't want mom and dad to know you rebounded from your breakup as fast as a racquetball off the wall."

"I did no such thing." She laughed.

"I think you did." Tina grinned. "Good for you." Her eyes brightened. "How was he? I think I could be happy just looking at him. I love Trevor but Adrian's body…"

She fanned herself again.

"I did not sleep with him."

"Just made out, huh?"

"No." She tried to look appalled but was pretty sure the heat in her cheeks was giving her away.

"Oh, so you tripped on a vacuum." Tina tugged her sweater away from her neck.

"Oh shit. You noticed that?" She pulled her shirt back up.

"How could I not. I can't believe you let him give you a hickey."

"I didn't let him. It's not like he asked." She stood and hurried to the mirror. "Do you think mom saw it?"

"Yep. Dad wasn't happy when he saw it, but mom calmed him down."

"When was this?" She hadn't noticed a thing.

"When you came in the house."

"All that happened when we came inside? And how did mom calm Dad down?" Their father wasn't hot tempered, but he was very protective of his kids, especially his girls.

"With a small touch. Watch them. Ever since they almost got divorced a few years ago, they've been different with each other. More loving." Tina sighed. "It's like they share secrets with every glance and touch and man, they touch a lot." She picked up a pillow and hugged it. "I want what they have."

"How did I miss all that?" She hadn't noticed anything.

"You were too busy glaring at your poor boyfriend like he'd betrayed you to your worst enemy."

"I thought he had. He wasn't supposed to come in the house. He wasn't supposed to meet the family." She looked at the wrapping paper. "He was a one-night stand that's all." But he'd remembered how much she liked wrapping paper and he'd been funny and nice and thoughtful and…Damn it, no. All alpha males started out that way. They'd do anything to get what they wanted and right now he wanted a repeat of last night. Her body hummed. It wouldn't mind that one bit.

CHAPTER 45: ADRIAN

Adrian parked the car in the yard at his parents' house. The large driveway was already overflowing with vehicles. It seemed that everyone had made it home this year.

Deb's three, young boys raced out of the house yelling, "Uncle Adrian's here! Uncle Adrian's here!"

As soon as he stepped out of the car, the kids barreled into him, their little arms wrapping around his hips and legs. "Hey, Merry Christmas. Help me carry the stuff inside."

"Yeah! Presents!"

"Yep." He popped the trunk, grabbing his gym bag as the kids snatched the bags of presents that he'd packed in the trunk before going to La Petite Mort Club last night.

The three boys ran to the house, passing their father, Roger.

His brother in-law stopped at his car, picking up a stack of boxes and said in a low voice, "Warning. Paige is looking for you and she wants a favor."

"Okay." He grabbed the remaining gifts and closed the

trunk. That wasn't too unusual. Paige was the youngest and spoiled. She always wanted something, but Roger would tell the story at his pace. He followed his brother-in-law toward the house in silence.

"The problem is Mary doesn't want you to do it."

"Why? What does Paige want?"

"Adrian, my favorite brother." Paige grabbed him as soon as he got near the door, pulling him inside.

"You'll find out," muttered Roger as he walked away dropping the gifts by the huge pile of presents under the tree.

Paige gave him a big hug, squishing some of the gifts. "Please, please tell mom that you'll go with me." She turned and glared at their oldest sister Mary. "Even though, I'm nineteen and I don't need a chaperone."

"Go where?" He pried himself free from his youngest sister and deposited the presents with the others.

"Ann Marie has tickets to this club on New Year's Eve and she invited me but Mary"—that one word was filled with enough venom to poison a rattle snake—"convinced mom that it isn't safe for me to go."

"It's not the place. It's the company." Mary's tone was icy enough to bring down the temperature in the room by several degrees.

"Who's going to be there?"

"Anne Marie's brother," said Mary.

"Anne Marie's...Oh." They had to be talking about Anne Marie's oldest brother Colin.

"Exactly." Mary sounded like she'd just won the

argument.

Colin was a year older than Mary and something had happened between the two in high school. Adrian was four years younger than Mary so the best he'd been able to put together was that they'd had sex. Colin had probably been her first and then he'd moved on. It was enough to infuriate him at twelve but not any longer. That shit happened with teens all the time. It sucked but guys were assholes sometimes. Mary should be mature enough now to understand that, but first loves left deep scars.

"It's not like Colin wants to go." Paige's green eyes gleamed mischievously. "Although, he is gorgeous. Maybe I could change his mind."

"And that's why you can't go," said Mary. "You're too much of a child to have the sense to stay away from men like him."

"I'm an adult and so is Anne Marie. It's ridiculous that we're only allowed to go with chaperones."

"Bad things can happen to adults." Mom came into the living room and hugged Adrian. "Glad you made it. Did you get your friend home?"

"Yes, I did, and her parents said to thank you and tell you"—he raised his voice so everyone could hear—"that you raised the kindest, most wonderful man in the world." Okay, he was exaggerating a bit but it was worth it to hear his sisters groan.

"Of course, we did. Now, tell me what you think about your sister going to this club?"

"Mom." By her tone Paige may as well have stomped

her foot. "I'm an adult."

"Do you pay for your college?" asked his father as he walked over and gave Adrian a hug. "Good to have you home, son."

Paige wasn't giving up. "No, but…"

Dad turned to his sister. "What about that college apartment you're moving into? Who pays for that?"

"You do." Paige was pouting now. She knew the argument was over.

"Then you're not an adult and you'll listen to your mother."

"Yes, Dad."

"Mary is against it, but she's never liked that boy Colin," said Mom.

"He's hardly a boy anymore, mother," said Mary.

"I told Paige she could go but only if you went with her," said Mom.

"I thought you wanted me home for New Year's Eve."

"I do." Mom kissed his cheek. "I want you home always, but I remember what it's like to be young." She glanced at her oldest daughter. "Unlike others."

"I think you mean young and stupid," said Mary.

"I meant what I said and if Adrian goes, he won't let Paige be stupid. Just young."

Paige pleaded with him silently, her eyes begging him while Mary glared at him, threatening retribution if he sided with their younger sibling.

"What club?" He wasn't in the mood to babysit his sister and a group of her friends, but family was family.

"The Blue Newb," said Paige. "Please, Adrian. Say yes. It just opened. It's almost impossible to get tickets."

Mary could retaliate all she wanted because he was going to that club. Fate had once again stepped in and he never argued with destiny, especially when it was on his side.

Get A Banging New Year and find out what happens next.
https://ellisoday.com/books/a-banging-new-year

Or find out what happens and save some money by purchasing the boxset
https://ellisoday.com/books/hot-holidays-books-1-3

Thanks for reading *The Mistletoe Game*

(Hot Holidays Book 1)

Keep reading for a peek at the next time Ellie and Adrian meet.

A BANGING NEW YEAR (HOT HOLIDAYS BOOK2)--EXCERPT

Adrian made his way across the club, his eyes never leaving Ellie. She looked gorgeous. Her hair was pulled up in some sort of messy bun that his fingers itched to undo. He wanted to watch those silky, soft tresses tumble down over her breasts—preferably, her naked breasts.

He knew the moment she saw him. Not only because the other woman forced Ellie's head his way, but because her eyes widened in surprise before she chugged her drink. Normally, he wouldn't take that as a good sign, but her eyes had also taken a quick trip down his body. She wanted him even though she'd pretend she didn't.

"Ellie." He stopped at the table and then turned his attention to the other woman. "Alison?" They'd never met but this had to be Ellie's friend who he'd spoken with on

Christmas during the car ride to Ellie's parents' house.

"Adrian." Alison pushed out the chair between her and Ellie. "It's so great to actually meet you in person. Join us."

"I'm sure he's busy," said Ellie.

"Not at all." He started to sit.

"That's Harker's chair." Ellie grabbed it, trying to push it back by the table but Alison clung to the other side.

"Harker's not here," said Alison.

Adrian stepped back as the two played tug-o-war with the chair for a second before it slid toward Alison and almost knocked her off her seat.

"Sit." Alison shoved it toward him.

Ellie glared at her friend, but Adrian ignored her, sitting and sliding the chair a little closer to Ellie as he scooted it up by the table.

"May I buy you ladies a drink?" Their glasses were full, but it was always polite to offer.

"I'm good," said Ellie.

"You are that," he muttered.

"Shots," said Alison. "Let's do shots."

"Ah...sure." He waved at the waitress.

"I don't want a shot," said Ellie.

"Too bad. You need one." Alison turned to the waitress. "Bring us three shots of tequila."

"I'm not getting plastered just because you want to," said Ellie.

The waitress hesitated.

"Okay." Alison's eyes gleamed. "We'll play a game."

"What kind of game?" Ellie watched her friend like a

189

rabbit watched a snake.

"You have to drink a shot every time you're mean to Adrian."

"I like this game," he mumbled around his beer.

"I'm not mean to him."

"Ha. Still lying I see." This time he didn't mumble.

"I'm not lying, and I'm not mean to you." Ellie elbowed him in the arm.

"You are too," said Alison.

"And you're mean to Harker."

"She is that." The man who'd been at the table with the two women earlier pulled out a chair on the other side of Alison and sat.

"I'm not mean to you. Sticking up for myself is not the same as what she does." Alison sent Ellie a smug look.

Adrian looked at Harker. The man was as amused as he was, and the other guy was definitely interested in Alison so tonight was perfect. "I'm Adrian and she's very mean to me." He held out his hand and the other man shook it.

"Harker."

"How many shots?" asked the waitress, growing impatient.

"Bring a shot glass, a bottle of Jose 1800, limes and salt." Harker handed her his credit card.

"We don't sell by the bottle."

"You do to me." Harker pointed over her shoulder where a dark-haired guy in a suit was talking to a table of women. "Verify it with your manager."

"Okay." The waitress left.

"Now, let's establish the rules for this game," said Harker.

"Ellie drinks every time she's mean to Adrian," said Alison.

"And Alison drinks whenever she's mean to you," said Ellie.

"I'm not…"

Harker touched Alison's lips. "Shut up for one second, okay?"

Adrian winced. His sisters would've bitten off the man's finger and torn out his eyes for that, but Alison just bristled, slapping Harker's hand away.

"I'll presume there'll be some contention over what's classified as mean so we'll vote." Harker's eyes met Adrian's with a clear message. If they worked together, they'd always win because the women were working against each other.

"Sounds good to me." He tipped his head slightly, letting the other man know that he understood.

"And when do you two drink?" asked Ellie.

"When we're mean to the two of you." It seemed simple to him and perfect because he had no intention of being mean to Ellie.

"That's not fair. You're never mean to me because you want to get me back into your…." Ellie stopped, her face heating.

"No reason to hide it. I think we all know what's on the table." Harker's dark gaze drifted to Alison, but she didn't even notice.

The waitress came back and put the shot glass, limes, salt and full bottle of tequila on the table. She handed Harker his credit card.

"Keep our other drinks full too." Harker gave her a couple of bills and at least one of them was a hundred.

"Yes, sir." She strolled away.

Alison opened the tequila, poured it into the glass and slid it to Ellie. "Drink. You were mean to Adrian."

"I was not."

"You were," he whispered none too quietly.

"When?"

"As soon as I walked over to your table."

"I wasn't mean." Ellie glanced at Harker. "I didn't want Alison to give away your seat." She smiled softly and Adrian was pretty sure she was batted her eyelashes. "So, it was actually Alison who was mean to you." She slid the shot across the table to her frenemy.

Adrian wasn't letting her get out of this so easily. "She didn't even say hi. I hadn't seen her since I drove her all the way to her parents' house on Christmas and she couldn't even say hi to me."

"Is that true?" asked Harker.

Ellie's mouth opened and then shut. Even she knew she'd lost this one, but she wasn't going down without a fight. "Yes, but only because I didn't want him to take your seat."

"That wasn't mean," said Harker.

Ellie smiled but Adrian sent the guy a look that said –

what the fuck? They were supposed to be on the same team.

"It was rude." Harker pushed the glass toward Ellie and picked up the bottle. "And that's two drinks."

"Still want to save his seat?" Alison burst out laughing.

"Okay, but he"—Ellie pointed at Adrian—"drinks whenever he's cocky."

"Now, wait one moment." That was a dangerous rule. He was always cocky.

"That's the only way I'm playing." Elle gave him a challenging look.

"Don't be a pussy," said Harker. "You can't be that arrogant."

Adrian shrugged. "Obviously, you don't know me very well, but I'll play. I like tequila."

Get A Banging New Year and find out what happens next.
https://ellisoday.com/books/a-banging-new-year

Or find out what happens and save some money by purchasing the boxset
https://ellisoday.com/books/hot-holidays-books-1-3

Keep reading to see how Ethan and La Petite Mort Club helped to save Liz and Craig's marriage.

Or maybe you want to meet more of the gorgeous and kinky men and women of La Petite Mort Club.

Just check out the excerpts. There's one for the

following books:

A Merry Masquerade for Christmas. Craig and Liz are headed for a divorce over a misunderstanding. Can one night of kinky fun at a masquerade ball save their marriage?

His Sub (free ebook) — Terry's a dominant but Maggie's not his usual sub. She's a curvy, single mother of three who needs a dominant's guidance more than any woman he's ever met. However, she insists on fighting him every step of the way..

Interviewing for her Lover (free ebook) — Nick's the consummate playboy. Sarah is looking for a lover for a few nights. They should be perfect for each other and they are. Too perfect. Their chemistry is off-the-charts explosive. Will they be able to walk away after only six nights of fantasies? (this book is the first of their six nights together).

The Voyeur (free ebook)–See how Patrick (Adrian's boss) and Annie meet. She's a maid who likes to watch people having sex at the Club. He's given the job of keeping her out of trouble, but he's the biggest danger to her because no matter how hard he tries, he just can't keep his hands off her.

Plus, if you sign up for my newsletter, you can get the entire Six Nights of Sin series for free (all six nights of

Nick and Sarah's contract—every delicious fantasy) as a thank you gift.

Click here to join and get your free book.

Here's What You Get When You
Join My Readers' Group

Win Before You Can Buy
Exclusive Giveaways
Free Books
Sneak Peeks

Go to my website or email me for details:

www.EllisODay.com

authorEllisOday@gmail.com

A Merry Masquerade For Christmas

Liz shoved the mop across the floor. She always cleaned when she was upset. Her house was going to be spotless. This was all so unfair and so typical. Craig was going to a party—a masked party on Christmas Eve. She'd be sitting home, crying and watching *It's a Wonderful Life,* while her husband would be having the time of his life with some other woman. She snorted. Nothing new there. He'd been doing it for years.

Her phone beeped. That'd better not be him needing something else. She'd skewer him with the mop handle if she had to see him again.

She put the mop down and walked into the kitchen to grab her phone. Damn, he'd looked good yesterday—his body strong and lean, his dark brown hair a little too long. When she'd turned and he'd been looking at her with desire…no hot lust, she'd almost fallen into his arms. She hated that she still wanted him. He'd never change. He'd always cheat—her father had, her sister's husband had. Craig wouldn't be any different, especially with a membership to that club.

She grabbed her phone off the counter and stared at her messages. This had to be a mistake, but it wasn't. It was a blessing.

Come and check out The Christmas Eve Bash. Mask Required. Clothing Optional. Doors open at 6 pm. Non-members show this message for entry.

This had to be the party Craig was attending. Ethan must've forgotten to remove her from the potential client list. It was her own Christmas miracle. She hurried to the garage. She had to find a mask. She was going to show Craig that she wasn't just his wife—soon to be ex-wife. She was a woman who needed a man and she was still attractive enough to get one.

Find out what happens next.
https://ellisoday.com/books/a-merry-masquerade-for-

christmas/

Free - His Sub

Terry wandered through the crowd of well-dressed women and men at La Petite Mort Club. It was the same scene every time Ethan, his friend and owner of the Club, threw one of these events. The members mingled with the newbies, hoping to snag something different or someone interesting.

Ethan strolled casually toward him, a ready smile on his face as he greeted his guests. "Terry, about time you made it down here."

"Like you can talk." His friend spent most of his time

in the back office, watching the Club on monitors.

"I've been mingling for over an hour."

"It's your business not mine." He leaned against the balustrade, peering down on the crowd.

"True, but you could sell your practice and buy me out."

"And run this place?" He laughed. "No thank you." He tossed back his scotch. "I spend enough time here as it is." He used to practically live here except when he was at the office or in court, but lately he'd been staying home more.

"Good turn out tonight." Ethan waved at a waitress and a moment later they each had another drink.

"Yeah, but I don't see one interesting person in this crop of wannabe members."

"And you can tell if someone is interesting just by looking at them?"

"I can tell not one of them has an original thought. Look at them. They're all in red." The Club was awash in a sea of red dresses—short, long, dark, light but always red.

"It is a Valentine's Day party."

"I know but you'd think one woman"—he held up his finger—"one would consider that everyone else would be in red and wear a different color."

"There are some pinks out there."

"Same thing, just lighter."

Ethan grabbed his phone from his pocket and looked at the text, frowning.

"Problem?" The Club was usually a safe place but on open night events, when Ethan allowed non-members access in order to recruit new members, the place could get dangerous.

"A little skirmish over a woman." Ethan grinned, his blue eyes sparkling as a couple of young guys hurried past them, almost tripping in their haste to stay close to a group of very attractive women. "These youngsters haven't learned that sharing is more fun."

He ignored Ethan's teasing. He'd taken a lot of shit from Ethan, Nick and even Patrick because he wasn't into the sharing thing. He preferred it to be him and one woman, one sweet, little sub. Since he was in no mood to listen to any more crap, he'd change the subject. "Those kids barely look old enough to drink."

"You're showing your age." Ethan patted his shoulder. "You should find some nice, young thing and teach her how to please her master."

"Maybe I will, if any of them show enough originality to dress in something other than red."

"I've got to go and sort out this problem." Ethan slid his phone into his pocket. "I'll find you later. If you find that elusive non-red dress, I'd suggest we share but..." He chuckled as he headed down the stairs, maneuvering through the crowd like he had nowhere to go, when in reality he was heading for the back—the playrooms.

Terry's eyes stopped and lingered on the new hire, Desiree, who was moving around the room, talking and flirting with all the men and some women. She was interesting—exotic and smart—but there was a shrewdness behind her eyes that he'd learned a long time ago to avoid.

A woman like her had an agenda and she stuck with it, no matter what.

Someone slammed into his back, causing his drink to spill down his front, staining his shirt and suit.

"Oh…oh, I'm so sorry."

He spun around and encountered a red dress and breasts—milky white and lush. The skin would be fragrant and softer than rose petals.

"Oh. Your shirt. Let me get something to wipe that up."

He forced his eyes away from those lovely breasts. Her hair was a rich mahogany. It'd probably hang past her shoulders in waves of curly silk but right now it was piled haphazardly on her head in what had been some kind of elegant style before disobedient strands had escaped their restraint. She looked mussed and damnit, he wanted to be the one to muss her.

"Paper towels? Napkins?" She glanced around and then hurried over to the bar.

She was short and curvy—her body succulent, ripe and he'd bet juicy. She grabbed a stack of napkins and headed for him. Her dress was too tight, like she'd recently gained some weight. He usually went for the tall, athletic types but for some reason his dick had picked this woman.

She returned to his side and dabbed at the wetness on his shirt and jacket as if she actually gave a shit about his clothes. This was no subtle caress, no flirtation—just indifferent efficiency.

"I'm so sorry." She wadded the napkins in her hand,

still patting at his clothes.

"You said that already." His words came out gruffer than he'd meant. No one treated him with disinterest. He was a rich, successful, attractive man and she was treating him like a child. He wanted to pull up her—unfortunately, red—dress and fuck her right here. They were at the Club. It wasn't out of the question.

Her hand froze. "Oh." Her large hazel eyes looked startled and then hurt. "Sorry. Ah, excuse me." She headed toward the stairs, dropping the wet napkins in the trash before disappearing in the crowd.

He turned around, so he could see the first floor and waited for her to appear. She hurried across the downstairs room, bumping and stumbling through the crowd. A lone, scared, little rabbit in a room full of predators. She stopped for a moment, scanning the crowd as if searching for someone.

"Who are you looking for, little rabbit?" he mumbled to himself. "A husband? Boyfriend?" He grinned as he lifted his scotch to his lips. "Girlfriend?" He frowned at the empty glass. "You spilled my drink. I'll forgive you, but it's going to cost you." He waved at one of the waitresses. "Everything has a price, little rabbit." As one of the best divorce lawyers in town, he knew that better than anyone.

The waitress brought him another drink. He paid, giving her a large tip before turning to find his little rabbit. He took a sip of the scotch, enjoying the smooth burn and his lush little bunny's journey through La Petite Mort Club. She froze in her tracks, her jaw dropping open as she gazed at a threesome on one of the couches.

The woman was sandwiched between two men, stroking one's cock as the other man fondled her beneath her red dress. The man behind her looked up and said something to the little rabbit. Her face heated and Terry's eyes dropped to her chest. Yep, they were a pretty shade of pink but what he really wanted to know was if the color matched her pussy.

She stumbled away from the threesome, bumping into another man. It was Richard, who stopped her from falling and then immediately let her go, stepping away. She was safe with Richard. As a member of the Club and a gentleman, he knew that safewords were law and consent was absolutely necessary. She said something to Richard and continued through the Club, disappearing in the crowd.

"You're not getting away that easily." He followed along on the upper floor, keeping her in sight. He had no idea why but he wanted her. Maybe it was simply because she was different than everyone else here.

He took another sip of his drink. It was obviously the little rabbit's first time at a place like this but she didn't seem eager to participate or interested in watching. She truly seemed to be looking for someone specific—not just someone to fuck. Well, she'd found the latter because he was going to fuck her. In the office he followed his head but at La Petite Mort Club his cock was king.

She headed toward the playrooms. There was no way he was going to miss this. He sauntered down the stairs, grabbing another drink on the way. She wasn't hard to follow. She left a path of irritated people in her wake as she bumped into them and apologized profusely before hurrying forward. Her full, round hips swayed under her tight, red dress that'd seen better days—hem frayed and at least five years out of style. Not that he minded, especially the snug fit of the cloth, but his women were usually much more put tougher.

They were the CEO types—women who thrived on being in charge. He enjoyed teaching them how much fun turning over control could be. When they were with him, he was their dom, their master and he made sure they loved every second. He told them when to kneel, when to suck, when to spread their legs or ass and when to come. The more power they had in their everyday life the more they craved bowing to his wishes. His little rabbit wouldn't know what power was. She was a hot mess of a woman. Still, his dick wanted her, so his dick would have her.

She was hurrying out of the first playroom when he entered the hallway. Her eyes were huge and her cheeks were on fire. She ducked into the next room and quickly came out—even redder than before.

"Excuse me." He'd offer his assistance in her search. She'd be grateful. He could capitalize on that unless she was looking for her husband or boyfriend. He wasn't in the mood to share. He would, however, allow the other man to watch. He could give the guy some pointers on how to take care of his wife because this woman obviously needed guidance.

"You?" Her eyes narrowed.

That wasn't the reaction he was used to. Women usually purred for him.

"Are you following me?"

"What would you do if I said I was?" He took a step toward her.

"I'd scream. There are bouncers here. I saw them."

Lord, she was cute. "Yes, but if they came running at every little scream they'd die of exhaustion."

As if to emphasis his point a woman screamed in ecstasy. His little rabbit's face heated and she averted her gaze.

"Who are you looking for?" He ran his finger lightly down her cheek. Her skin was as smooth as porcelain but much warmer and softer.

"Ah…" Her breath hitched, making her breasts swell dangerously above her gown.

He could have her out of it in a minute. The skin would be even softer than that on her face. "Did you lose your husband?"

"No." She licked her lips.

There was no way he could let that offer pass. He slowly bent, giving her time to refuse him. He may command his women but he made sure they always wanted it first. Her eyes dropped to his mouth and he couldn't help a slight smirk. She wanted this as much as he did. He moved closer and let his lips rest gently on hers. He'd take it slow, make her yearn for him and then he'd make her obey.

"What are you doing?" She turned her head.

"Kissing you." His lips brushed against her cheek. He wasn't about to lose ground.

"Why?" She turned again, her eyes meeting his.

The confusion in her hazel gaze was as obvious as the hideous dress on her gorgeous body. She may remind him of a rabbit but she couldn't be that naive. She had to be in her mid to late thirties.

He should use flowery words—tell her she was beautiful, desirable—but that wasn't him. Blunt was the kindest word to describe him. "Because, I want to."

"You don't even know me."

He was losing ground. The interest in her face was being replaced with disgust. "No, but I know I want you." Damn, he shouldn't have said that.

"Well, too bad." She pushed on his chest and he stepped back, letting her pass.

"This is a sex club, you know." He followed. "If you aren't here for sex, why are you here?"

She spun around. "I'm quite aware of what this place is and just because I don't want you, a stranger to…to"—she waved her hand about—"in the hallway."

He laughed. "We wouldn't be the first. There are people fucking in the main room."

"I know. I saw." Her cheeks heated.

He stepped closer. "You are adorable." He touched a strand of hair that was resting on her shoulder. It was like satin.

"I'm a mess." She pulled her hair free from his fingers.

"A hot mess. A fiery, hot, sexy mess." He moved

closer with every other word. "One I want to fuck, right now."

Her eyes hardened. "Too bad because I don't"—again she waved her hand about—"you know, with strangers in the hallway." She shoved his chest again.

He took a small step back but he wasn't giving up yet. "We can go to a private room."

"No."

Shit. By the look on her face, he'd just made a bigger blunder.

"Let me go." She pushed him again.

Damn. She'd said the worst three words in the English language besides I love you. He moved away, releasing her for the moment. "Sorry."

She harrumphed.

"I made a mistake."

"Yes, you did." She hurried down the hallway but not before he'd seen the look of hurt in her large eyes.

"What the fuck do you want from me? I made a mistake and apologized." He trailed after her.

"I want you to leave me alone. Please. Go away."

He stopped. His little rabbit was running but perhaps, he shouldn't chase. She darted down a hallway toward the hardcore BDSM rooms.

Normally, she'd be fine—embarrassed but fine. Except with all the newbies here, tonight wasn't a normal night. He hurried after her. "Hey, I don't think you want to go—"

"Leave me alone." She walked faster. "I need to find my friend and get out of here."

"Okay, but I don't—"

"Go away." She sounded both mad and as if she were going to cry.

"Suit yourself, but I warned you."

She strode into the closest room. He should leave. Let her find out that he wasn't the worst thing in a place like this, not in a long shot, but his feet followed her. She was his little rabbit. He'd found her. No one else was going to enjoy her until he'd had his taste.

"Vicky? Vicky? Are you in here?"

He stepped into the room, staying in the shadows. She was looking around in the dark for her friend. It only took a moment for one of the six guys to notice the little rabbit who'd stumbled into their den.

"Shit," he mumbled. Not one of those guys was a regular.

Grab your free copy and find out what happens next.
You can find the book on my website
https://ellisoday.com/books/free-his-sub/

Free: Interviewing For Her Lover

"Do I have to take off my clothes?" Sarah tugged on the hem of her black dress. It was shorter and lower cut in the front than she normally wore, but the Viewing was about finding a man for sex and according to Ethan men liked to look.

"No." Ethan turned her away from the door and forced her to look at him. "You don't have to do anything you don't want to do."

She stared into his blue eyes. Why couldn't he be interested in her? She'd only met with him five or six times, but she trusted him. He ran his business, La Petite

Mort Club, very professionally and he was gorgeous with his sandy brown hair, strong cheekbones and vibrant blue eyes. Sex between them would be good. Easy. He was attractive and...not for her. She didn't want decent sex or good sex, she wanted mind blowing, screaming orgasms and that wouldn't happen between him and her because there was no chemistry, no attraction.

"Listen to me." He moved his hands to her shoulders and gave her a gentle shake. "You aren't selling yourself to the highest bidder. You're looking for a partner. One who'll"—he grinned—"turn you on in ways you can't even imagine."

She glanced at the door where the men waited. Waited for her. Waited to decide if they wanted to fuck her. "I'm a bit nervous."

"About what?"

This was embarrassing, but she'd been honest with him up to this point. She'd had to be. He was helping her...had helped her to choose the five men in the other room. "What if none of them..."

"They will want you." He touched her chin, turning her face toward him. "A few of them may back out after this but not because they don't want you."

"Yeah, right."

"I'm only going to say this once. You're beautiful and different, unique."

"That's not necessarily a good thing." She had long legs and a nice body—trim and firm—but with her auburn hair and green eyes she was cute at best, not gorgeous. The men she'd chosen were all rich, good looking and powerful. They could have anyone they wanted.

"It's exactly what they want, or most of them anyway." He took her hand and led her closer to the door.

She leaned on his arm, hating these shoes. She should've stuck with her flats but Ethan had given her a list of what she should wear and high heels were on the top. She'd found the smallest heels in the store and by Ethan's look when he'd first seen her she might've been better off going barefoot. He'd met her at the private entrance and his gaze had been appreciating as it'd skimmed over her dress until he got to her feet. Then he'd frowned and shook his head.

"Finding the right men for you wasn't easy." He stopped at the door.

"Thanks a lot." She shifted away from him, his words hurting a little. She hadn't been sure of her appeal to the opposite sex in a long time, not since the early years with Adam.

"It's not because you aren't beautiful but because you want to be dominated and you want to dominate—"

"I do not want to dominate." All she could picture was a woman in black leather with a whip and that wasn't her, not at all.

"If you say so." He smiled a little. "But, you do want to lead the scene. Right? Because that's what—"

"Yes." Her face was red. She could feel it. She didn't want to talk about her fantasies again. It'd been embarrassing enough the first time, but he'd had to know what she wanted to compile a list of candidates.

"Most at the club are either doms or subs. Very few are switches." His eyes raked over her. "That's what's so special about you. You want it all and…that's what made choosing these men difficult."

He'd given her a selection of twenty-two men who might be interested in what she wanted. She'd narrowed it down to seven. Two had been uninterested when he'd approached. That'd left her with the five who'd see her in person for the first time tonight, but she wouldn't see them. That'd come after the Viewing when she interviewed any who were still interested.

"Remember what you want. This is your deal. You call the shots. At least a little." He kissed her forehead. "But don't refuse to give them anything. You don't want a submissive."

"No." That didn't turn her on at all and she only had eight weeks. One night each week for two months before she'd go back to her lonely life, her lonely bed, dreaming of Adam.

"You can do this." He pulled a flask from his jacket and unscrewed the lid. "For courage."

"Thanks." She took a large swallow, the brandy too thick and sweet for her taste but it was better than nothing.

"Now, go find your lover."

She laughed a little but sadness swept through her. There'd be no love between this man and herself. This would be sex, fucking. That's all. The only man she'd ever love, her only lover, was dead. This was purely physical. "Thank you again." She stood on tip-toe and kissed his cheek. He may be gorgeous and run a sex club but he was a good man, a good friend.

She turned and opened the door and walked into the room, trying to stay balanced on these stupid heels. Men wouldn't find them so attractive if they had to wear them. The room was dark except for one light highlighting a small platform. That was for her. She stepped up onto the small stage. The room was silent but they were there, above her, hidden behind the one-way mirrors, watching and deciding if they wanted to take the next step—to eventually take her.

She stared into the blackness of the room. It wasn't huge but its emptiness made it seem vast. She glanced upward, the light making her squint and she quickly stared back into the darkness. This was arranged for them to see her. That was it. She'd get no glimpse of them yet. She'd seen their pictures, chosen them but meeting them in person would be different. A picture couldn't tell her their smell or the sound of their voices.

She tugged at her dress where it hugged her hips, wishing the questions would start, but there was only silence. She shifted, the heels already killing her feet. Ethan hadn't liked them and if they weren't going to impress, she might as well take them off. She moved to the back of the stage, leaned against the wall and removed her shoes. As she returned to the center of the stage a man spoke, his voice loud and commanding almost echoing throughout the room.

"Don't stop there. Take off your dress."

She bent, placing her shoes on the floor. That wasn't part of the deal. She wasn't going to undress in front of five men, only one. Only the one she chose. She straightened. "No."

"What?" He was surprised and not happy.

"I said no. That's not part of the Viewing."

"I want to see what I'm getting."

She stared up toward the windows, squinting a little. She couldn't tell from where the voice had come. The speaker system made it sound as if it were coming from God himself. "And you will if I pick you."

Another man laughed.

"It's not funny. She's disobedient," said the man with the loud voice.

"Not always. I can be obedient." These men liked to be in control but sometimes, so did she.

"Will you raise your dress? Just a little," asked another voice.

"Didn't you see enough in the photos?" She'd applied a few months ago for this one-time contract. She'd been excited and nervous when she'd received the acceptance email with an appointment for a photography session. She'd never had her picture professionally taken, since she didn't count school portraits or the ones her parents had had done at JCPenny's. She'd been anxious and a little turned on imaging wearing her new lingerie in front of a strange man, so she'd been disappointed to find the photographer was an elderly woman, but the lady had put her at ease and the photos had turned out better than she'd expected. She glanced up at the mirrors, hoping she wasn't disappointing all the men. That'd be too embarrassing.

"Those were…nice, but I'd like to see the real thing before deciding if you're worth my time."

She raised a brow. "You can always leave." She shouldn't antagonize him. She was sure the bossy man had already decided against committing to this agreement. Disobedience didn't appeal to him. That left four. If she didn't pick any of them, she could go through the process again, but she didn't think she would.

The man chuckled slightly. "I know that, but I haven't decided I don't want to fuck you. Not yet, anyway."

The word, so harsh and vulgar excited her. It was the truth. That was what she, what they were all deciding. Who'd get to fuck her. It was what she wanted, what she'd agreed to do, and as much as she dreaded it, she wanted it. She was tired of being alone. She missed having a man inside her—his tongue and fingers and cock.

"Do any of you have any questions?" She clasped her dress at her waist and slowly gathered it upward, displaying more and more of her long legs. She ran. They were in shape. The men would like them.

"Lower your top," said the same man who'd told her to take off her dress.

She didn't like him. If he didn't back out, she'd have Ethan remove him from her list. He was too commanding. He'd never allow her to be in control.

"I don't know if he's done looking at my legs yet."

She continued raising the dress until her black and green lace panties were almost exposed.

"Very nice and thank you," said the polite man.

"You're welcome." This man might work. She shifted the dress up another inch before dropping it, giving them a glance at her panties.

"Now, your top," said the bossy guy.

She lowered her spaghetti string off one shoulder, letting the dress dip, but not enough to show anything besides the side of her bra.

"More," he said.

"No." She raised the strap, covering herself. She didn't like this man and wished he'd leave. She'd kick him out but that wasn't part of the process and they were very firm about their rules at this club.

"He got to see your pussy. Why don't I get to see your tits?"

"You got to see as much as he did." She was ready to move on. She bent and picked up her shoes. "If there's nothing else, gentleman, we can set up times for the interview process."

"Turn around," said another man.

It was a command, but she didn't mind. There was a politeness to his order and something about the texture of his voice caused an ache between her thighs. There was a caress in his tone but with an edge and a promise of a good hard fuck.

"Are you going to obey?" His words were whisper soft and smooth.

"Yes." That was going to be part of this too. Her commanding and him commanding. She dropped her shoes and turned.

"Raise you dress again."

She looked over her shoulder at where she imagined he sat watching her.

"Please." There was humor in his tone.

She smiled and slowly gathered the dress upward. She stopped right below the curve of her bottom.

"More. Please." There was a little less humor in his voice.

She wanted to show him her ass. She wanted to show that voice everything but not with the others around. This would be just her and one man, one stranger. That was one of her rules. "No. Only if you're picked do you get to see any more of me than you have." She dropped her dress, grabbed her shoes and walked off the stage and out the door.

She was going to have sex with a stranger. She was going to live out her fantasies for eight nights with a man she didn't know and would never really know, but she wasn't going to lose who she was. She'd keep her honor and her dignity which meant she had to pick a man who'd agree with her rules.

Get your free copy and find out what happens next.

https://books2read.com/u/3nYKo6

Free: The Voyeur

Annie finished making the bed and gathered the sheets from the floor, keeping them as far away from her body as possible. These sex rooms were disgusting and Ethan was a jerk making her work as a maid. She almost had her Bachelor's Degree in Culinary Arts, but he'd refused to hire her for the kitchen—too many men in the kitchen. The only job he'd give her at La Petite Mort Club was as a maid and unfortunately, she needed the money too badly to refuse.

She stuffed the dirty sheets into the cart and hurried out the door. She had almost thirty minutes before she had to be at the next "sex room." She hid the cart in a closet and darted down a back hallway, staying clear of the cameras. Julie, the woman who supervised the daytime maids, was a real bitch. If she were caught sneaking away from her duties, she'd be assigned to the orgy rooms every day. Right now, they all took turns cleaning that nightmare. She swore they should get hazard pay to even go in those rooms.

She slipped through a doorway and hurried to the one-way mirror. She stared at the couple in the next room. From her first day here, she'd been curious about the activities at the club. She was twenty-four and wasn't a virgin but she'd never, ever done some of these things.

The woman in the room below was tied to a table, legs spread and wearing some sort of leather outfit that left her large breasts free and her crotch exposed. She had shaved her pussy and her pink lower lips were swollen and glistening from her excitement. The man strolled around the table as if he had all night. He still had his pants on but had removed his shirt. His arms and chest were well defined but he had a slight paunch. His erection tented his pants and Annie felt wetness pool between her legs. She had no idea why watching this turned her on but it did. Ever since she'd accidentally barged in on that guy and girl in the Interview room, she couldn't stop watching.

The man below ran his hand up the woman's inner thigh, glancing over her pussy. The woman thrust her hips upward and Annie ran her own hand between her legs. The man's mouth moved but Annie couldn't hear anything and then he slapped the woman across the thigh hard enough to leave a red mark. Annie jumped. She wasn't into that, but she couldn't stop watching the woman's face. At first, it'd contorted in pain but then it'd morphed into pleasure. The man hit her again and then bent, kissing the red welts— running his tongue across them as his fingers squeezed her nipple.

Annie clutched her thighs together, searching for some relief. Her panties were soaked. It wouldn't take but a few strokes to make her come. She started to slide her hand into her pants.

"Having fun?" asked a deep voice from behind her.

She spun around, her heart dropping into her stomach. "Ah...I was just finishing cleaning in here." Damn, she should've closed the door but she hadn't expected anyone in this area. The rooms were off limits on this floor until tonight and she was the only one assigned to clean here.

He shut the door and locked it before strolling toward her. She'd seen him around the Club, but more than that she remembered him from the military photos her brother, Vic, had sent to her. She carried one of the three of them—Vic, Ethan and this guy, Patrick—in her purse. He'd been attractive in the picture, but now that he was older and in person he was gorgeous. He had dark green eyes, brown hair and a perfect body. He stopped so close to her his chest almost brushed against her breasts. She was pretty sure it would if she inhaled deeply. She really wanted to take that deep breath and feel his hard chest against her breasts.

"Don't let me stop you from enjoying the show."

"I...I wasn't. I should go." She started to walk past him but he grabbed her hand.

His grip was warm and strong but loose enough that she could pull free if she wanted. She didn't. Even though she only knew him from her brother's pictures and letters, she'd had many fantasies about him when she'd been in high school. Her gaze dropped to the front of his pants and her mouth almost watered. He was definitely interested. She dragged her eyes up his body, stopping on his face. He smiled at her.

"There's nothing to be embarrassed about. Watching turns us all on." He kissed the back of her hand and she jumped as his tongue darted out, tasting her skin.

"I...I should go." She didn't move.

"No, you should watch." He dropped her hand and grabbed her shoulders, gently turning her toward the mirror. He trailed his hands up and down her arms. "Watch."

The man in the other room was now sucking on the woman's breast as his fingers caressed her pussy.

"Would you like to hear them? Or do you like it quiet?" His voice was a rough whisper against her ear.

"Sound, please." She wanted to hear their gasps and moans. She wanted to close her eyes and pretend it was her. She shifted, squeezing her thighs together.

He chuckled as he moved away. She felt his absence to her bones. He'd been strong and warm behind her and for a moment she'd felt safe, safer than she had since her brother had come back from the war, broken and sad, and her father had started drinking again.

The woman's moans filled the room and Patrick came back to stand behind her, this time placing his hands on her waist.

"I'm Patrick," he said against her ear.

She couldn't take her eyes from the scene in front of her. The woman was almost coming as the man thrust his fingers inside of her.

"What's your name?" He nipped her neck and she jumped.

"I...I..." If she told him her name, he might say something to Ethan. Ethan would kill her if he knew she was in here watching.

"Tell me your name." His lips trailed along her neck and she tipped her head giving him better access.

The guy was kissing his way down the woman's body. Annie wanted to touch herself, to make herself come but Patrick was here.

He nibbled her ear. "Why won't you tell me your name?"

"I...I'll get in trouble." She rubbed her ass against his erection, hopefully giving him a hint.

"Tease." His hand drifted down her stomach, stopping right above where she wanted him to touch. "Tell me your name or I'll make you suffer." He unbuttoned her pants and left his hand—warm, rough but immobile—resting on her abdomen.

"I can't." She stood on tip-toe, hoping his hand would lower a little but he was too tall or she was too short. He had to be almost six foot and she was barely five-foot four. "I could get fired and I need this job."

"Darling, Ethan won't fire you for fucking a customer."

"We can't." She spun around. She hadn't thought this through. He was her fantasy come to life and she wanted him to be hers just for a moment, but Ethan would find out and then she'd be in deep shit.

"Don't worry. I'm a member and you work here, so we're both clean." He hesitated, his hands tightening on her hips. "Are you protected?"

"What?" She had no idea what he was talking about.

"Ethan makes sure everyone at the Club is clean but only the…some of his employees are required to be on birth control." He ran his hands up her sides, getting closer and closer to her breasts. "Are you on birth control?" His eyes darkened as they dropped to her tits. "If not, it's okay. There are other things we can do."

Oh, she wanted to do everything his eyes promised, but she couldn't. "No, I'll get in trouble. I need this job. I have to go." She tried to move but her feet refused to obey, so she just stared at his handsome face.

"Are you sure?" He bent so he was almost eye level with her. "I promise. Ethan won't care. A lot of maids become…change jobs. The pay's a lot better." His eyes roamed over her frame. "Especially, for someone as cute as you."

Ethan would kill her before letting her become one of his pleasure associates.

"I could talk to Ethan for you." His hands moved up her body, stopping right below her breasts.

Her nipples hardened and she forgot everything but what he was making her feel. He ran his thumb over one of them and she leaned closer, wanting him to do it again.

He did. He continued rubbing her nipple as he spoke. "I could persuade him to let me…handle your initiation into club life."

Her heart raced in her chest. It could be just her and him doing all these things she'd seen. Her pussy throbbed but she couldn't do it. She wouldn't do it. She couldn't have sex for money. Her parents were both dead but they'd never understand and she couldn't disappoint them. "No. I can't do that…not for money." Her eyes darted to the door. She needed to get out of there before she did something she'd regret.

"That's even better." He smiled as he stepped closer. "We can keep this between us. No money. Only a man and a woman." He leaned down and whispered in her ear, "Giving each other pleasure. A lot of pleasure. In ways you haven't even imagined."

There were moans from the other room and she glanced over her shoulder. The man's face was buried between the woman's thighs.

Patrick turned her around, pulling her against him and wrapping his arms around her waist. "Are you wet?"

"What? No." She struggled in his arms, her ass brushing against his erection again.

"Oh fuck. Do that again." He kissed her neck, open mouthed and hot.

She stopped trying to get away. She wanted this…this moment. She shouldn't but she did, so she wiggled her butt against him again. He was hard and long and her body ached for him. It'd been too long she'd had sex. She needed this.

"Would you like me to touch you?" His hands drifted over her hips and down her thighs.

She'd like him to do all sorts of things to her. She nodded.

"Say it." His words were a command she couldn't disobey.

"Yes."

"Yes, what?" He untucked her shirt from her pants.

"Touch me. Please." She was already pushing her hips toward his hand. She wanted his hand on her, his fingers inside of her.

"Are you wet?" he asked again.

She inhaled sharply as he unzipped her pants.

"Don't lie to me. I'll find out in a minute."

She'd never talked dirty during sex and she wasn't sure she was ready to do that with a stranger. Her heart skipped a beat. Maybe, she shouldn't be doing any of this with a stranger. She grabbed his hand. "Maybe, we shouldn't."

The woman below cried out and the man straightened, wiping his face and unbuttoning his pants.

"Watch. The main event is about to happen." Patrick's hot breath tickled her neck.

Her gaze locked on the man's penis. It was large and demanding. He straddled the woman, grabbing his cock.

"Don't you want to feel some of what they feel?" He nibbled on her ear and then neck. "I can help you."

She may not know him, but she trusted him. He was a former marine. He'd been a good friend of Vic's. He wouldn't hurt her and she needed to come. She loosened her grip, letting go of his hand. He slipped inside her pants, caressing her pussy through her underwear. His fingers were long and strong. She closed her eyes, leaning against him as he stroked her.

"You're already so wet and hot." His breath was a warm caress on her ear. "But, I'm going to make you wetter and then, I'm going to make you come." His other hand shoved her pants down, giving him more room to work. "Open your eyes and watch the show."

She did as he said. The man was inside the woman, thrusting hard and fast. The woman was moaning and trying to move but the restraints kept her mostly helpless.

"Fuck, you're soaked." Patrick's hand cupped her and she arched into his touch, rubbing her ass against his erection. He shoved his hand inside her underwear, his finger running along her folds until he slipped one inside.

"Oh." She grabbed his hand—not to push him away, but to make sure he didn't leave.

He smiled against her hair. "Don't worry, baby. I won't stop." He stroked his finger inside of her and his wrist brushed against her clit.

She needed more. She needed to touch him, feel him. She turned her head, wrapping her arms up and around his neck. He kissed her. It was desperate and wild, but he stopped too soon.

"They're almost done. You don't want to miss it."

She turned back to the mirror. The man below continued to fuck the woman as Patrick finger-fucked her. His other hand slipped under her shirt to her breast. His lips sucked her neck as he rocked his erection against her ass. He was everywhere, and she was so close. The muscles in her legs constricted. Her hips tipped upward.

"Wait, baby," he groaned in her ear, as he pushed a second finger inside of her. "Just a few more minutes."

His fingers were stretching her and it felt wonderful. She moaned, long and low as he thrust harder and faster, almost matching the pace of the man in the other room. She could almost imagine it was Patrick's cock and not his fingers inside of her.

"Oh…oh," she cried out. He was pushing her toward the edge. Her body was spiraling with each pump of his fingers. She was going to come—right here while watching that couple. It was so dirty and so wrong and it only made her hotter.

The woman below screamed and her body stiffened. The man thrust again and again and then grunted his release.

"Show's over." Patrick nipped her neck at the same time he pressed down on her clit with his thumb, sending her shooting into her orgasm.

She trembled and he pulled her close, his hand still cupping her pussy and his fingers still inside of her. When her heartbeat had settled, he removed his hand and bent, pulling off her shoes and removing her pants before lifting her and carrying her to the wall.

"My turn." He wrapped her legs around his waist.

Her phone rang. "My work phone. I…I have to answer it."

"When we're done." He unzipped his pants.

"Annie, answer the phone. I know you're around here. I can hear it ringing you stupid bitch," yelled Julie.

"Oh, shit." She shoved Patrick away, and ran across the room, grabbing her clothes off the floor. "It's my boss. She'll kill me if she finds me like this."

"I'll take care of Julie." He headed for the door, zipping up his fly. "Don't move." He grinned over his shoulder at her. "You can take off your pants again, but other than that, don't move."

"No. Please." She raced over to him, grabbing his arm. "I need this job." And Ethan could not find out about this.

"She won't fire you. She can't. Only Ethan can fire you." He bent and kissed her.

His lips were gentle and coaxing this time and her body swayed into him. He pulled her even closer and she could feel his cock, thick and heavy, pushing against her. Her pussy tightened again in anticipation.

"Damn it, Annie. This is going to be so much worse if I have to call your stupid phone again. Get out here!" Julie was only a few doors down.

She grabbed Patrick and tugged on his hand. "Please, hide." She glanced around, looking for somewhere that would conceal a six-foot muscular man.

"I'm not going to hide from Julie."

Get Your FREE Copy and find out what happens next.

HTTPS://BOOKS2READ.COM/U/BXQBMK

BOOKS BY ELLIS O. DAY
OR SEE THEM ALL ON MY WEBSITE
HTTPS://WWW.ELLISODAY.COM

LA PETITE MORT CLUB SERIES

THE BILLIONAIRE'S BABY
https://ellisoday.com/books/the-billionaires-baby
The Baby Bargain (book 1) (free)
https://books2read.com/thebabybargain
Making the Baby (book 2)
https://ellisoday.com/books/making-the-baby
The Baby Battle (book 3)
https://ellisoday.com/books/the-baby-battle
Having the Baby (book 4)
https://ellisoday.com/books/having-the-baby

HOT HOLIDAYS
Hot Holidays -The Complete Series: Books 1-3
https://ellisoday.com/books/hot-holidays-books-1-3
The Mistletoe Game (Book 1) (free)
http://mybook.to/mistletoegame
A Banging New Year (Book 2)
https://ellisoday.com/books/a-banging-new-year
Cupid's Misfire (Book 3)

https://ellisoday.com/books/cupids-misfire

SIX NIGHTS OF SIN SERIES
Six Nights of Sin -The Complete Series: Books 1-6
https://ellisoday.com/books/six-nights-of-sin-books-1-6/

Interviewing For Her Lover (Book 1) **(Free)**
https://books2read.com/u/3nYKo6
Taking Control (Book 2)
https://ellisoday.com/books/taking-control
School Fantasy (Book 3)
https://ellisoday.com/books/school-fantasy
Master-Slave Fantasy (Book 4)
https://ellisoday.com/books/master-slave-fantasy
Punishment Fantasy (Book 5)
https://ellisoday.com/books/punishment-fantasy
The Proposition (Book 6)
https://ellisoday.com/books/the-proposition

THE VOYEUR SERIES
THE VOYEUR **(FREE)**
https://books2read.com/u/bxqBMk
Watching The Voyeur (Book 2)
https://ellisoday.com/books/watching-the-voyeur
Touching The Voyeur (Book 3)
https://ellisoday.com/books/touching-the-voyeur
Loving The Voyeur (Book 4)

https://ellisoday.com/books/loving-the-voyeur

The Voyeur Series (Books 1-4)
https://ellisoday.com/books/the-voyeur-series-books-1-4/

SIX WEEKS OF SEDUCTION
https://ellisoday.com/books/six-weeks-of-seduction

A MERRY MASQUERADE FOR CHRISTMAS
https://ellisoday.com/books/a-merry-masquerade-for-christmas/

THE DOM'S SUBMISSION SERIES
The Dom's Submission Box Set (Books 1-3)
https://ellisoday.com/books/the-doms-submission-books-1-3/
His Sub (Book 1) (**Free Ebook**)
https://books2read.com/u/3yrBlV
His Mission (Book 2)
https://ellisoday.com/books/his-mission/
His Submission (Book 3)
https://ellisoday.com/books/his-submission/

LA PETITE MORT CLUB INTIMATE ENCOUNTER SERIES
YOU KNOW THE PLAYERS, BUT DO YOU KNOW THE KINK?

HIS LESSON (TERRY AND MAGGIE)
https://ellisoday.com/books/his-lesson/

PLAYING HOUSE (NICK AND SARAH)
https://ellisoday.com/books/playing-house

HIS LOVE (TERRY AND MAGGIE)
https://ellisoday.com/books/his-love/

HIS IMPERFECT DAY (TERRY AND MAGGIE)
https://ellisoday.com/books/his-imperfect-day

COMING SOON:

ETHAN'S STORY

HARKER and ALISON'S STORY

MATTIE'S STORY

JAKE'S STORY

REBECCA AND DEREK'S STORY

VIC'S STORY

Email me with questions, concerns or to let me know what you thought of the book. I love hearing from readers.
authorEllisOday@gmail.com

https://www.EllisODay.com

Follow me

Facebook
https://www.facebook.com/EllisODayRomanceAuthor/

Closed FB Group (sneak peeks, sample chapters, and other bonuses)

Ellis O. Day

https://www.facebook.com/groups/153238782143373

Bookbub
https://www.bookbub.com/authors/Ellis-o-day

Instagram
https://www.instagram.com/authorEllisOday/

Twitter
https://twitter.com/Ellis_o_day

Pinterest
www.pinterest.com\AuthorEllisODay

ABOUT THE AUTHOR

Ellis O. Day loves reading and writing about love and sex. She believes that although the two don't have to go together, it's best when they do (both in life and in fantasy).

Ellis O. Day

www.ingramcontent.com/pod-product-compliance
Lightning Source LLC
Chambersburg PA
CBHW050737180626
46814CB00002B/792